# COSMIC TREASON

## UNIVERSAL WILDERNESS: BOOK THREE

### FREDRICK NILES

FEVER GARDEN PUBLISHING

COSMIC TREASON

First edition. October 26, 2022.

ISBN: 978-1-950021-15-4

Fever Garden Publishing

Cover design by

TheCoverCollection.com

❀ Created with Vellum

## PROLOGUE

Captain Dennis Kane watched through the viewport as the debris of Desia's automated defense system drifted by. The hunks of stone and metal that had once consisted of the numerous defense frigates and automated cannons lay suspended in the black like silt at the bottom of the ocean. The viewport's diamond reinforced glass was so thick that not so much as a *tick* could be heard as the shattered pieces knocked into the ship passing through the debris field.

When the Peoples Union Coalition fleet had entered the Pillon System through the Void Gate, they were quickly engaged by Desia's defense apparatus. Consisting mostly of automated cannons built into the asteroid field that lay between the gate and Desia, the Pillon System's core planet, the defenses were quickly dispatched. The people here weren't interested in fighting a war. Most of them just wanted to escape the law. The law had come however, and now ship-after-ship could be seen fleeing the war zone.

A loud *boom* shuddered through the vessel as some of the crew barked into their comms. Kane ignored them.

Down below, the planet of Desia looked calm. Serene. Dense jungle green broken up by huge stretches of dark blue, all underneath the undulating patches of white and grey that made up the planet's weather system. From up here, it almost looked small. Fragile. Peaceful.

Kane knew that wasn't the case. He had doubted it at first—had thought the screams that came pouring over the comm units were some separatist ploy meant to redirect focus from the full-scale invasion the PUC had launched less than fourteen hours ago.

But now he knew that he had been wrong. Desia wasn't peaceful down below. The screams had been genuine. And while the PUC had launched the invasion, they were no longer the aggressors.


IT HAD STARTED WITH ONE.

One body was all it took. In hindsight, Kane actually considered himself lucky. Fresh off of shore leave, military vessel 9FC-4253 had been docked for the last 5-days at Space Port Alpha. Alpha was one of the largest ports in all of known space and was located just adjacent to Lydia, the PUC's capital planet. 4253's crew was refreshed. Their food stocked. The Light Core they used to power the ship swapped out for maintenance. But most importantly, their onboard morgue had been emptied.

Located directly behind medical, a ship's morgue was often the most overlooked area. But being a military vessel, there was never any shortage of opportunities to use the cold dand sterile freezer section that housed all the dead bodies the ship accumulated over the course of its journey. Not all of them were combat fatalities. Vessel 9FC-4253 housed a crew of about 10,000 and it was far from the largest in the fleet. Many of the fatalities could be attributed to things like accidents, medical emergencies, and the occasional brawl that got out of hand.

4253 had only been out of port for 2 hours before a young cadet named Phillip Grenny had dropped dead of a massive cerebral aneurysm. The death had been shocking to those who knew the young man. Kane hadn't known him personally but he had served with his father some decades ago in the Centralization War.

A full-scale planetary invasion couldn't be stopped by the untimely death of a single person however, and the ship passed through the Void Gate with the rest of the fleet that had been docked at Station Alpha.

It was the other ships that had more to worry about. While most of the vessels had been recently staffed and loaded up with supplies and munitions, nearly a quarter of the attacking fleet had come from other occupied systems.

And some of their morgues were full.

From what Captain Kane was able to piece together from the onboard surveillance system, a pulse of energy originating from the surface of Desia had surged through the ship. It had felt strange—like the shadow of some unseen predatory bird flashing overhead before it could be glimpsed—but that had been all. No sparking panels or blown out thrusters. Hell, the lights hadn't even flickered. It had just been that feeling. Or so they had thought.

When the pulse wave hit, the recently deceased Cadet Grenny transformed. Not yet put on ice, his body lifted off of the gurney he had been temporarily placed on, the jet-black body bag still wrapped tightly around him. The form hung quivering in the air like a poltergeist, no one to observe it but the security cam in the back corner.

Long, serrated legs pierced the quivering bag, the fabric

tearing open to reveal something so repellent that the captain had to resist the temptation to turn the recording off. Part crab and part scorpion, the thing skittered out of the room, knocking trays and empty gurneys aside in a tremendous clatter.

That's when the bodies had really begun to pile up. 4253 had sent most of its armed soldiers down to Desia's surface to secure critical locations, but most of the remaining crew were still armed. It had only taken two minutes and seventeen seconds to bring the creature down, but it had been so fast and so lethal that before it finally lay twitching in a bloody mess on the ground, it had impaled, dismembered, decapitated, and disemboweled its way through 23 crew members.

Kane didn't even hear about it until it was over and by that time he had already heard the cries for help from his soldiers on the ground. It sounded bad down there, and not just bad, it sounded like Hell. That's why he had been so skeptical at first. The reactions had been so over the top—so desperate and guttural that he thought someone had hacked their comms and were playing mind games with them.

Then he saw the footage. He saw how the thing ripped through armed men and women like they were paper. He saw and he believed.

Now he was standing at the viewport, watching a large storm system make its way east over one of Desia's massive oceans. The bridge had been sealed off, the entire ship put on alert. They had hailed the others nearby and received no response. Of course they hadn't. Some of those ships were from places like the Onyx System or Polfax. They had been in literal war zones before being diverted here and their morgues had probably been full to bursting. Who knew how many of those things were running around up here. Especially now.

The first pulse wave had been unexpected and had cost them the lives of 23 good men and women. But the second wave had been catastrophic. Kane had felt his stomach jump up into his mouth as the second wave crawled through the length of the vessel. For the first time in his life, he actually prayed—prayed to whoever would listen that it didn't mean what he thought it did.

And as his worst fears were confirmed, he felt his stomach slide back down. Lower and lower until it felt like his guts would be pulled right through the floor. He thought he might faint. Might throw up. But he did neither.

Instead he watched. Captain Dennis Kane watched the security feed as the 23 new monsters turned the corridors of his ship into a goddam meat grinder. And as he watched, he tried to think of a plan. He had immediately sealed off the vital sections but the creatures were already pounding on doors, prying their way into air ducts, and finding weak points in the walls to dig through. At this rate, he would either have to evacuate, blow up the ship, or both.

The problem was that the PUC didn't take kindly to either of those things. This was a momentous occasion in history. They had come here to secure the final star system and connect it to civilization. They couldn't fail, and they especially couldn't abandon their posts. Not to mention the fact that they had nowhere to go. Hell, there were probably more of those things on the ground than there were up here. Plus, there was a good chance that any of the people they

ran into down there would be hostiles. The PUC *had* come
to invade their star system after all.

There was no answer. No plan. No way out. So instead,
Kane just watched. And as he did, the darkness of night
slowly crept over the planet's surface far below.

1

———

## DOWN IN THE DARK

Branches and vines whipped past Vanessa Jackson's face as she tore her way through the underbrush. The sun had just dipped below the horizon, bathing the sky in deep crimson, but the dense jungle canopy turned twilight into pitch black. There should have been animals chirping and hooting around her—the large Marpana Apes that swung through the trees or the tiny swarms of Flapper Bats that made wet slapping sounds as their leather wings beat the air—but there was none of that now. The jungle held its breath and the only things that Vanessa could hear were her pounding feet, her beating heart, and the sound of a thousand breaking branches as something ripped through the trees behind her.

Vanessa's sides screamed in pain where, earlier that day, she had been repeatedly kicked and beaten by the PUC's Minister of Defense, Seamus Clark. He was dead now. The last she had seen of him, he was eviscerated and bleeding out on the cement floor of the Light Wire facility he had come to power up.

That had been the whole reason the PUC had invaded:

the Light Wire. They had come to connect Desia and the rest of the Pillon System into the PUC's information transfer grid and thus secure a monopoly on all communication that passed between star systems. When it had been engaged however, something went wrong—something piggy-backed on the signal—something alien. Something from the Void.

The Void was a dimension without light and without time. It was how people traveled from system to system and it was supposed to be empty. Apparently, it wasn't. When the Light Wire was turned on, something resembling music had been pumped through. In reality, it was like nothing Vanessa had ever heard before. Sounding like a combination of gulping and scraping, she thought she had imagined it, laying half-conscious from her beating on the floor. But then the second wave hit. The song wasn't audible this time, but when the pulse wave passed through her, the song was there all the same. In her head. In her soul.

There was no denying its transformative power. Something in the signal caused dead flesh to mutate. Dead *human* flesh, as far as she could tell. She didn't know how, but the monsters that were chasing her had come from that pulse wave—from the dead bodies the PUC had created and then the fresh new bodies that had been torn apart after that. Regardless of how strange and alien they looked, Vanessa now had to face the fact that the dead walked the earth.

And not just walked but sprinted. The things behind her were fast. She had seen them move over open ground and it was like watching a fly dodge a swatting hand. The monsters' reflexes were honed, their bodies agile. The only reason she was still alive was that they seemed to have a hard time powering their big bodies through the dense jungle brush. Vanessa had spent the better parts of her life dashing through the jungle and she knew how. She had an instinct for it. The monsters though were just big enough to get caught in branches and hang up. They could eventually tear themselves free but only after a struggle.

Vanessa's body ground to a halt and she stood there in the dark listening, trying not to drown out the sound of her surroundings with her labored breathing. The night was silent. Nothing moved. She doubted that the monsters had stopped pursuing her though. They were probably hunting her at that very moment. Following her scent or sound or who the hell knew? Maybe they could see perfectly in the dark. They were from the Void after all.

A twig snapped some thirty feet behind her and Vanessa felt the hairs on the back of her neck prickle. Something big was moving through the brush. She crouched lower, trying to make herself invisible. The jungle air was thick and humid. Sweat ran down her face and stung her eyes. She pressed them shut, composing herself.

The sound of a ship engine suddenly roared overhead as it passed, shattering her calm. She actually yelped at the sound and, realizing her mistake, immediately threw herself into motion. The bramble seemed thicker now and moving forward felt like a slog, as if she were trying to run on a planet with twice the amount of standard gravity.

She ducked. She didn't know how she knew, but her body must have felt it—must have expected it. All she knew was that in one second she was desperately struggling through the brush and then she was flat on the ground as a razor-sharp limb scythed through the air over her head and separated the trees just in front of where she had been standing. Had she not acted instinctively, she would likely be nothing more than a headless corpse right now.

Vanessa actually felt tears in her eyes as she scrambled

away, her hands and knees pounding the moist jungle floor. Once again, she couldn't hear anything but her desperate flight through the wilderness. Couldn't see half a foot in front of her face. She was blind and deaf and if she continued on this way she would either be torn down to nothing by the scratching branches or her heart would simply explode inside of her chest.

And even as she pushed herself back to her feet and continued her blind dash through the forest, she knew she was lost—knew that it was only a matter of time before they caught up to her or she literally stumbled into one. She pushed on anyway.

Then all of a sudden, she was pushing against nothing. The brush evaporated along with the ground beneath her and there was nothing but the night air and the slice of red sky above her like a knife-wound in the very world itself. She hung there for an elongated moment, her every nerve feeling as if they were expanding, her body frantically searching. A ledge, a ladder, a helping hand. But there was nothing. There was only the empty air and the gravity that yanked her down through it.

The fall was mercifully short: less than ten feet. But when she hit the ground her ankle folded sideways against a rock like a piece of soft cardboard. Red hot agony sliced up her leg as she crumpled into a heap on the ground and she screamed in pain without a single thought for what heard her.

It appeared as if she had found a small rock quarry dug into the jungle. Off to her right lay a large abandoned bulldozer and beyond that, the bulbous nose of a civilian class freighter stuck out around the corner. It was doubtful that the thing still ran, but if she could just get inside...

She took a labored step forward, putting as little weight

on her ankle as possible. She made it one step and then two more. Time seemed to turn to sludge. Any second those things could burst out through the trees and cut her down. She picked up her pace.

Step, *drag*. Step, *drag*.

She heard the sound of shifting rubble behind her and didn't have to look. Something was on the ledge watching her. She moved faster.

Step, *drag*. Step, *drag*. Step, *drag*.

She was halfway to the bulldozer. It wasn't perfect but it was something. If she could just make it to the other side, then she'd have something to put between the monster and herself. And if there were more than one? Well, she'd have to figure that out when the time came.

Step, *drag*.

She was *so close*.

Step, *drag*.

All of a sudden there was a furious clatter of hard exoskeleton feet hitting stone as something dashed up behind her. Vanessa tensed, waiting for the hot knife of pain from being cleaved in half. She saw another shadowy figure scrabble down the rocks off to her left and then another crouched down by the bulldozer.

Blue light erupted in front of her as the sound of gunfire ripped the world open. An ear-rending screech pierced the night as Vanessa felt hot blood spray the back of her neck. She froze. Half from pain and half from shock. Tiny blobs of light continued to dance in her vision as she tried to let her eyes adjust, but then the energy rifle flared again, tracing a straight line of impossibly bright blue light between the figure by the bulldozer and the monster that had just finished descending the ridge of the quarry.

Vanessa wanted to shout. To question. She wanted to

give thanks at the same time she demanded to know who was there. She never got the chance.

She caught the movement out of the corner of her eye. Long spindly limbs racing over the quarry floor. The thing leaped up into the air, becoming practically invisible against the night sky, and by the time she was able to see it again, it was bearing down on her. Then in the last second, a blue light crackled to life off to her left.

The light sliced up through the air in front of her and neatly bisected the front third of the monster. Momentum carried the body forward and the dead weight of it sent Vanessa and her savior crashing to the ground in a tumble of limbs.

"*Phuu*," she spat, clearing the thing's blood from her mouth. She looked around wildly, trying to orient herself.

There was movement off to her right as a man slowly got to his feet. He appeared to have a long blue sword of crackling electricity coming right out of his hand. There was a noise off to Vanessa's left and her head spun.

A large armored figure materialized into the blue light of the burning sword, its faceplate opaque and assessing. It reached out a hand.

"Vanessa Jackson." The voice belonged to a woman and was slightly modulated as it came through the helmet. "Nadia Yahantov of the Leopold. I believe we spoke on the radio."

Relief flooded through Vanessa. Before she had escaped the Light Wire facility, she had desperately flipped through a series of radio channels trying to find someone still in the air that might be able to level the structure. She had been able to reach a few of the PUC ships orbiting Desia but they were either skeptical or outright hostile towards her. Just before she could lose hope entirely, she came across the signal that her daughter's ship, the Leopold, was on. Her daughter, Byzzie, hadn't actually been on the ship—she was hopefully hunkered down somewhere with the rest of the crew—but Nadia had been. The two of them had had a short exchange and minutes later, the Leopold obliterated the building with a Tesla Round.

She had hoped that it would work—that destroying the facility would shut off the signal the Light Wire had transmitted and that all of the monsters that had come with it would either drop dead or at least not gain any more brothers or sisters. She had been wrong. Just seconds after the Light Wire was destroyed, another pulse wave hit Desia and animated the group of dead bodies she had been standing by.

"Thanks," Vanessa said as she was pulled to her feet. She gingerly tested her ankle. It hurt but it didn't feel like a break. "You really saved my ass there."

"We picked you up on thermal after blasting the Light Wire." Nadia tilted her head toward the dead creature lying less than a foot away. "Picked these things up too."

"You actually outran a good number of them," added the man who had just gotten up. The blue saber retracted back into his hand with a snap. "Maybe 'outran' isn't the right word, but it seems as if these things have a short attention span. The others lost interest and bounded off in the other direction pretty quick. They probably couldn't make it through the thick brush."

"Kittredge, I assume?" Vanessa asked, stretching out a hand. She noticed that the man was missing his right hand. In its place was the metal black nub that the saber had come from. Vanessa could also make out a thick cord of wiring snaking up the man's arm to wrap around his back.

"Correct. I assume you recognize your daughter's work." He held up the device attached to his forearm.

"She'd mentioned a while back that she had made a saber beam from a Tesla Arc. I thought it was a part of your suit though, not your arm."

"It was," he responded. "But I lost my hand a few weeks ago and she rigged this up for me. My suit got trashed when we tried to lift off this morning and come get you folks so I had to rig this up." Kit half turned to reveal the bulky shape of a Tesla Arc housing strapped to his back.

"When you say your suit 'got trashed,'" Vanessa said, "Is that why you weren't able to come pick up Byzzie and the others?"

"Yes, ma'am. We ran into an SEU squad. We shook 'em but my armor basically got cut in half in the process."

"Enough chit-chat," Nadia cut in. "I don't like standing out in the open like this."

"Sure thing," Kit said. Then to Vanessa: "Ship's just over here."

"Where are we going?"

Nadia turned toward Vanessa, hefting the rifle in her arms. "To find your daughter."

---

RAQUEL FIRED AGAIN AND AGAIN, the pistol jumping in her hand as she emptied her magazine into the monster before her. The heavy 10mm rounds punched through skin and bone, burst eyeballs, and tore off hunks of flesh, but the monster still came.

The medical storage facility that Raquel and half of her crew had taken shelter in had escalated into full-blown chaos. Screams and gunfire fought for dominance in the sonic landscape as the creatures pushed further and further inside, hellbent on killing every last living thing in the building.

49, the android that Raquel had recently been forced to call "crewmate" aboard the Leopold, had called them Necrosarks. Mutating from dead flesh, Raquel had watched a dead woman transform before her very eyes.

She had barely made it out alive.

Not that it mattered now. She was currently trapped halfway up a metal staircase with the monsters approaching from either side. The sound of an energy rifle blared above her as a small contingent of Desian militia members fought off the assailants approaching from the roof. They had succeeded so far, but in the back of her mind, Raquel wondered how long they could hold out.

The real weak point was here though. Right in front of her. Already weighed down by the unconscious body of an elderly woman she had sought to rescue when the fighting started, Raquel was pinned down with nothing but a pistol.

*Blam, blam, blam.* The gun jerked up into the air with every pull of the trigger. Holding it one-handed wasn't ideal, but unless she wanted the old woman to slide off her shoulders and tumble some twenty feet down to the ground below, she'd have to make do.

The thing hissed and clacked its huge mandibles as a round took out another one of its glistening black eyes. There was a clatter as it stumbled backward, its deadly limbs scrabbling for purchase on the staircase. Raquel lined up for another shot and felt the gun click uselessly in her hand. Turning it sideways, she saw that the slide was locked back. The gun was empty.

"Raquel!" Came a voice from above. She didn't need to turn to know who it was. King, the ship's mechanic had been plodding up the stairs on a wounded leg in front of her when they were attacked. She had hoped that he would continue upward without her, but apparently not. She shouldn't have been surprised; he was possibly the most stubborn man she had ever met.

"King, stay back." Raquel reached back to keep him from coming down but there was a loud metal thump as he dropped down onto the step behind her.

"Keep going," he said. "I got this."

Raquel threw a glance over her shoulder and saw that he was beat-red and slick with sweat. He had been on some sort of pain killer when the attack had occurred, but he had taken a Necrosark limb straight through his thigh. She didn't doubt that there was both muscle and skeletal damage, and if that was the case then it would be hard to quell the pain with a single dose of whatever he had taken.

"You don't *got this*," Raquel said desperately. Down below the creature she had wounded was regaining its composure.

"Just *run*, woman," King said as he shoved around her. She had to clamp down to avoid having the unconscious woman fall from her arms.

Raquel stared as King half-ran, half-stumbled down the steps. She wanted to run. Wanted to offer up the old woman as a sacrifice, grab King, and bolt in the opposite direction. But she didn't. She was dead anyway. Despite King's distraction, the things were everywhere. The only way she could go was up, and even if she made it past all of the other frightened people who were packed together on the steps above her, the only thing she'd find was another horde of monsters.

It was hopeless and it was over.

King bellowed as he swung a heavy fist at the monster's

head and to Raquel's amazement, the creature actually recoiled from the blow. King looked down at his fist in bewilderment.

*Did that just happen? Is King going to beat this thing in a fist fight?*

But just as Raquel began questioning everything she knew, the creature recoiled again without King even swinging at it.

No, not recoiled. It was being *pulled*.

The Necrosark threw its head back and screeched as it tried to turn around. And as it did, a lone figure was revealed behind it.

Down near the bottom of the steps was a large pale man wearing dirty white underclothes and holding onto the Necrosark's tail as if he was playing the world's most dangerous game of tug-o-war.

"Is that all you got?" Yelled the stranger.

Wasting no more time, the creature leaped off the edge of the stairs and as it did its tail was yanked out of the man's hands. Landing nimbly on its feet, the Necrosark immediately sprinted over the open ground at the man, its mandibles wide, forelegs raised for the kill.

Before it reached him however, a concussive *boom* echoed through the warehouse and a huge gout of black blood erupted from the creature's thorax. The Necrosark screamed and lurched sideways, its lower half breaking free and sliding to the ground as its guts spilled out. It collapsed into a heap and then tried to rise back up on its front legs. There was another boom, and this time the Necrosark's head split in half.

Before anyone could celebrate, three more came skittering across the ground, tails whipping in the air. The man down below spun to face them and it was then that

Raquel noticed the rifle slung over the man's back. Why didn't he use it?

It appeared he didn't have to though, because two of the three monsters were immediately cut down by tight bursts of energy fire from up above. Raquel spun to see who had fired and as she did, she saw a huge armored figure leap from the upper balcony.

The last Necrosark below had skidded to a stop and now raised its forelegs to meet the new attacker, its mandibles clacking furiously. The newcomer plummeted a hundred feet through the air like a giant stone, its heavily armored frame hitting the creature feet-first like a hammer blow. Black blood sprayed in every direction as the thing's exoskeleton shattered on impact.

Raquel stared in shock at the incredible display of power. She had wondered at first how a lone man might be able to pull one of those monsters off-balance with nothing but his bare hands, but now she knew. It was because he wasn't a man at all. He was a Surgical Equalizing Unit.

SEUs, or "Marauders" as they were sometimes called, were the PUC's elite killing force. Biomechanically enhanced, they were stronger, faster, and a hundred times more durable than any normal human being. Throw in above-average weaponry, intense training from birth, and heavy-duty power armor and they were near-unstoppable.

Raquel would know. After all, two of her crewmates, Kit and Nadia, were Marauders gone AWOL. That was the problem though. Kit and Nadia had deserted the PUC to live a life in exile. These soldiers hadn't and however much they had just saved everyone's asses, they were still PUC.

The nearly-naked man down below watched as the armored SEU stood up, wiping the creature's insides off his armor. The thing beneath him quivered and clicked its mandibles. It was still alive, just barely. The SEU lifted his big iron boot and stomped the Necrosark's face into the ground, its head exploding with a thick squelch.

"You run out too?" The unarmored man said as he unslung the rifle from his back. He popped the mag and looked at it.

"Yup," said the armored soldier. The voice belonged to a man and was slightly modulated.

"Told you we would. There's a fucking *lot* of these things closer to town."

"Well, thankfully we got Pollie covering us with the 50."

"Thankfully indeed. I was almost hamburger there," the half-naked man said. Then, slowly, he turned his gaze upward to Raquel and the others. The sounds of battle had ceased and as Raquel felt a part of herself relax, she couldn't help but wonder if they hadn't just traded one devil for another.

**2**

———

**RITZ**

The flashlight beam on the end of Ritz's energy rifle cut the darkness, illuminating stacked boxes of cleaning supplies, non-perishable food items, and office materials. The small storage closet had been locked but he had had the key. Or at least he had had *a* key—the key being a hyper-condensed 5.7mm energy bolt.

The PUC had hidden the supplies in the basement of a remote automated monitoring facility on the planet Lapharga. The facility had been guarded by a small contingent of combat synthetics, but luckily, Ritz and the other seven members of Kingsbane found that the same "keys" worked to deactivate those as well.

"Got some over here," Ritz called and Wesley Goff came jogging over. Goff was a large, intelligent man with a neck like a tree trunk and a pair of hazel eyes set deep within his skull as if to put as much space between them and the outside world as possible.

"Nice," Goff slapped Ritz on the shoulder. "I bet all these doors have supplies stashed behind them."

"Why do they have so much stuff here?" Ritz asked.

They hadn't actually come to Lapharga for supplies but to blind the PUC's presence on the planet. "I mean, why do they have so much *people* stuff. I thought this place was supposed to be fully automated."

"It is," Goff replied. "It's probably just a contingency in case some maintenance guy gets stuck here." He turned toward a group of men that were loading up the small lift that went up to the docking station where their ship was sitting. "Trevor. King. We got some more over here." Goff turned back to Ritz. "Why don't you go check the other rooms."

Ritz nodded and hurried off. The basement was narrow but long and winding. Ritz walked along blasting through the locks, checking every room. A few more had supplies while others just housed servers or maintenance hatches. Every time he found something worthwhile, he called to the others. If he just found servers or some other computer equipment?

Well, that was what the energy rifle was for.

Kingsbane was a large militia faction but it was fragmented by nature. Due to this, many of the groups had to make do with whatever supplies they could buy or steal. And that was certainly the case with Goff's crew. Possessing nothing but a crate of energy rifles and a small shuttle their pilot Hector had inherited from his dad, they were able to fly around creating small but meaningful instances of havoc for the PUC.

Unfortunately though, that meant they had no bombs, no C4, no Tesla Arcs, and definitely no Light Cores. So when they came across small facilities like this one, they had to sabotage them with small arms fire rather than simply blow it up.

When Ritz reached the last door in the farthest corner of

the facility, he only had a few rounds left. He looked down to confirm that the selector switch for his rifle still indicated single-fire. Then he put the rifle to his shoulder, lined up the iron sights with the center of the door's lock, and pulled the trigger.

The gun bucked against his shoulder and there was a loud metal pang as the energy bolt blasted through the locking mechanism and the door swung open.

Seeing movement, Ritz almost pulled the trigger again, but he stopped himself. Huddled in the corner of the small empty room was a tall and lanky man in a light blue jumpsuit and a pair of large-framed glasses. He reached over, trying to shield three children and a woman with his body. The children stared out from under the man's arms with large frightened eyes.

"Hey Ritz, we're almost done here," Goff called as he walked around the corner of the hallway. "Got anything else?"

"Nope," Ritz said, slamming the door closed. He tried to look up to meet his commander's eye, but couldn't. His gaze dropped back down toward his feet.

"You sure?" There was a note of suspicion in Goff's voice.

"Yup." Ritz forced his eyes back up. Goff's eyebrows were knit together, his brow furrowed. And in that moment, Ritz was transparent.

Goff pushed past him and opened the door. Ritz didn't stop him.

"Well," Goff said. "I guess we know what all those supplies are for."

Ritz turned and finally met his commander's eyes, pleading.

"They've seen our faces, Ritz." Goff's voice was gentle but

firm. "If we leave them here, they'll be questioned. Then the PUC will get sketches of us, they'll plaster them everywhere, and eventually someone is going to come knocking on our doors. So I'm going to make this easy for the both of us."

"Wait!" Ritz cried. He wanted to lift his rifle up and demand Goff to stop but he was too slow. Goff was already pulling his sidearm from the holster on his hip. He raised it up and pointed at the family cowering in the corner. Ritz wanted to scream. To beg. To reason. But he did none of those things.

THE SOUNDS of gunfire pulled Ritz back into the waking world. His body was covered in sweat and chills raced up and down his arms and legs. He tried to take a breath but when he did it felt like a car was parked on his chest. He looked down.

He was lying on a cot and was naked from the waist down. From his collar bone to the bottom of his ribcage was a large flesh-colored bandage with multiple wires running out of it and into a computer console at his bedside. In the center of the bandage was what looked like a giant silver bag that seemed to expand slightly as he inhaled and then depress as he exhaled. There was a terrible lag though, as if the signals his brain were sending to this new contraption were taking an exorbitant amount of time to get to where they needed to go.

Another blast of rifle fire sounded somewhere nearby followed by a scream and Ritz's head snapped up.

The room he was in had hospital equipment in it but was far from being a hospital room. An open ceiling revealed plumbing and electric. Along his right ran a bare concrete wall where other medical monitoring systems were plugged in and hooked up to unconscious patients. To his left lay steel racking full of wrapped pallets of medical supplies.

A massive boom echoed through the warehouse followed by another. There was the sound of something screeching and then more rifle fire and then it all came back to him.

Ritz had been shoved into an electrified cage along with most of the crew of the Leopold and some other prisoners. While contemplating how to get free, soldiers had dragged a boy to the cage and when the boy resisted and refused to go in, the soldiers had prepared to execute him. Ritz had fought back, managing to free himself and temporarily stave off the execution but then it all went south. The soldiers regained the upper hand, shot the boy, and then shot Ritz.

After that, there was nothing. Nothing but darkness and nightmares.

Ritz looked down at his bullet wound and as he shifted, pain shot down his right arm. Moving carefully, he observed another bullet wound, this one near his shoulder. It was less serious than the wound to his chest, but the pain persisted and as it did, Ritz realized that he had been given some sort of painkiller. And they were beginning to wear off.

The gunfire had ceased. There didn't seem to be any fighting going on any longer and Ritz hoped that whoever had won was on his side. He thought about screaming for help, but didn't want to draw attention to himself. If the rate at which the drugs were wearing off kept up then he'd be crying out soon regardless. He had some time though.

Trying to let his mind ease into the situation, he leaned back on his cot. The springs creaked and he groaned lightly as the sharp pain from his shoulder seemed to mix with the deep pain in his chest. He squeezed his eyes shut until he was fully reclined and then opened them again.

Thrashing involuntarily, he spilled out of the cot, sending it crashing to the ground. He screamed, half from the pain and half from what he had just seen.

Perched up on the wall was what looked like some sort of giant spider. With long, reaching legs, the spider creature slowly crept down the wall, its mandibles quivering.

Ritz tried to crawl away, but he hit the end of the wires he was attached to like a leash. A scream of pain surged up through his throat and this time he really let loose. Long and loud, the noise was somewhere between a cry of surprise and a sob.

He looked back up at the monster on the wall and realized with a jolt that it was mere feet away now. It was so close that he could see his reflection in its multitude of black eyes that were clustered near the top of its face.

Ritz opened his mouth, preparing to yell for the last time.

A long burst of energy rifle fire drowned out his voice. Black blood spattered the wall and floor beneath as the spider-thing fell thrashing to the ground. Ritz continued to scream as he kicked and crawled his way back. The sharp limbs flailed and stabbed the air in every direction as the creature died. Before it finally came to a stop, a lone silver figure stepped up and fired a quick succession of energy bolts into its face.

"49," Ritz managed, gasping for air. "What is—where are we?"

"You're safe," 49 said. 49 was an android and part of Ritz's crew. And while his allegiances had yet to be solidified, he had just made a few huge leaps in Ritz's opinion.

"What the fuck is that thing?"

"It's called a Necrosark," 49 explained. "It's a monster composed of dead flesh reanimated and reconstructed by Void energy. You're on the planet Desia. You were shot. We're now in a medical storage facility that has been transformed into a makeshift hospital. We just fended off an attack. I suspect—"

"Okay, okay," Ritz interrupted. "That's enough."

"I thought you wanted to know what-"

"I do," Ritz said, reaching up to rub his head. "Just not so...fast." Ritz looked past 49 and saw a group of children hiding around the corner of the steel racking. He nodded at them in question.

49 turned around to look at them and looked back. "Byzzie's siblings and a few other injured children. We were separated from the rest in the attack."

"And now you're reunited," yelled a loud male voice. Ritz craned his neck and saw a man dressed in nothing more than a white t-shirt and pair of undershorts. The clothing and the man's blonde hair were spattered with black blood and he appeared to have a rifle slung over his shoulder.

"Who's this?" Ritz asked, half to the man and half to 49. And before anyone could answer, an SEU wearing a full Arc Suit stepped around the corner with a heavily built dark-skinned woman wearing the same style of underclothes. Then another SEU climbed through a gap in the steel racking. Things began to click together.

"I believe these are our new..." 49 turned to look at Ritz and he had to give it to him: for an android he sure pulled off a wry expression well. "...*rulers*."

3
————

## CEASEFIRE

"A *what*?" The man across the table from Vanessa let out a bark of laughter. "A ceasefire? Oh, I'm sure you'd like that. Are you sure you don't also want us to get off this planet too? Maybe send some funding your way?"

"What I want," Vanessa said, steel in her voice, "Is for you to be tried for war crimes and executed along with every single person that stepped off of a PUC warship yesterday. That's what I *want*, Sergeant. But I'm willing to let you leave without so much as a scratch on that big chin of yours."

The man leaned forward. "And who exactly would be enforcing these war crimes? I don't see an army. Your minuscule defense fleet fled the moment we showed up."

"She doesn't need an army," responded Nadia from right behind her. "She just needs us."

Nadia stood tall and imposing in her Marauder armor. Kit stood just adjacent to her at the end of the table where 49 was sitting in an office chair they had wheeled in from one of the other rooms.

After the SEU team known as Indigo Squad had rescued

Ritz and the others from the medical storage facility in the center of town, Byzzie had rushed down the metal stairs, informing everyone that the Leopold had landed on the roof and would be transporting people to a secure bunker twenty miles south of the city.

The cargo section of the ship was tight and could only hold about a third of the people that had taken shelter in the warehouse. So Vanessa had gotten off and chosen to stay with Indigo Squad while Kit and Nadia had done three quick runs back and forth between the warehouse and the bunker. The third one had been the most interesting, seeing as Indigo was boarding a ship they had already been on.

"What the fuck is this?" James had blurted. They had just finished loading the last of the wounded onboard and were preparing to leave. James was the blonde-haired man who was still in his underclothes. He turned back to his squad-mates on the roof. "These are the assholes that killed Joaner."

"Well, I guess this is our ship now," said one of the armored SEUs. He raised his rifle and prepared to board. The two other SEUs prepared to do the same.

"Stop," Vanessa ordered, raising the sidearm she had procured from the Leopold's armory on the way over. Aside from 49, Indigo, and a few of the PUC soldiers who had taken shelter in the warehouse, they were the only ones on the roof. "We can't afford to be fighting each other right now. Those things could be back at any minute and I'm sure they'd love to find us killing each other."

"I think I'll take my chances with those things," said the armored SEU. "You may have noticed that we're not exactly helpless."

"Look..." Vanessa began and raised her eyebrows.

"James."

"Look James," Vanessa said. "How many SEU squads did you arrive with?"

James hesitated, still holding his rifle. Vanessa shot a glance toward the cargo hold that had its door open. There was a small contingent of PUC soldiers standing guard, clearly trying to decide whose side to take.

"Four," James finally said.

"Okay, four. And how many have you been in contact with since you landed?"

"One."

Vanessa waited a beat and then asked, "How many have you been in contact with *recently*?"

James was silent but Vanessa had seen enough. The two SEUs who weren't wearing armor said it with their body language. A slight shrugging of the shoulders. A furtive glance.

"You're not as invincible as you think you are," Vanessa explained. "Especially when half of you aren't wearing armor."

"Our fucking armor is onboard *that ship*," James blurted. "Those assholes stole it when they killed Joaner and booted us out the airlock."

"And why do you think they killed Joaner? Why kill him and not the rest of you?" No one answered. "It was because they were defending themselves."

"They wouldn't need to defend themselves if they didn't break the law," James responded. "The whole reason we're here is because this planet is full of a bunch of traitorous rats. In fact, I say we waste these guys and get the hell out of here. The planet's obviously fucked. Let's just burn the whole thing from space."

"Do you have the authority to make that call soldier?" The voice that spoke was raspy and weak, but not without an air of authority. Everyone turned to see an older grizzled man hobble into the light from the interior of the cargo bay.

"Colonel Hutchens," said the other armored SEU. Every soldier and SEU immediately snapped to attention, James never taking his eyes off of Vanessa.

"This is very clearly not the mission we signed up for," Hutchens said. He was hunched over and leaning against the edge of the cargo ramp door. He had a large bandage wrapped around his naked abdomen and appeared to be somewhat sedated. Even so, he didn't seem without his wits.

"The brass in the sky doesn't know what to do yet," Hutchens continued. "Half of 'em are fucking politicians, here to slurp up the glory when the taking of Pillon was all but certain. Now they're just trying to figure out the same thing you are: how to get the hell out of here without being court marshaled." He fixed his eyes on James. "So if you're still taking orders, *soldier*, then I recommend you listen up."

Everyone's attention was now firmly on the colonel.

"The captains on those ships in orbit need exactly one thing right now: a reason to leave. They can't do that unless the mission is no longer viable. The mission isn't unviable until Desia is completely burned down past the topsoil. And I mean *total* obliteration. They seem to be occupied with *something* at the moment—I don't know, maybe they're dealing with the same things we are—but eventually they're either going to start blowing infected vessels out of the sky or skip straight to a Tesla Bombardment. Then when they report back, they can say that ground forces were overrun so they had to resort to scorched earth tactics. They probably have footage of what's been happening by now, so the idea is actually feasible and able to be substantiated. So our clock is ticking."

"That's what I said though," James said, somewhat sheepishly. "Burn it from above."

"Not while we've got men on the ground, soldier," Hutchens barked, suddenly looking as healthy and uninjured as the rest of them. "You gonna let them turn this planet into a parking lot while you still have SEU squads down here? Your brothers and sisters?"

James's face flushed. If SEUs were known for one thing other than their hulking strength and abilities it was their dedication to each other.

"Fine," he said. Then he looked at the ship. "But as soon as we're done, these traitors are gonna get what's coming to 'em."

"SHE JUST NEEDS US." Nadia's words echoed through the conference room.

The room was stuffy and far too small for everyone packed inside. It had just been James, Vanessa, and Colonel Hutchens to begin with; but then Nadia and Kit had insisted accompanying them if they were going to be laying out tactical strategies. The rest of Indigo Squad couldn't abide having a ranking officer in the room with two rogue Marauders so now they were all in there as well.

James and Charlene, the other SEU that had been in her underclothes, had retrieved their armor from the Leopold and were now fully suited up except for James's helmet which he chose to keep off for negotiation purposes.

Finally, 49 had practically invited himself to the meeting, insisting that he had some pertinent information as to how to deal with the Necrosark problem.

So now, there they were. Eight people jammed into a

room meant for six at most, five of them wearing 800lb Arc Suits.

"What do you suggest, Colonel?" Vanessa said trying to avoid any more conversation with James. She still had to force the words out. The PUC was to blame for this whole thing. If they hadn't come here to activate the Light Wire they had secretly built then none of this would be happening. She hadn't even had time to check in with Byzzie and the rest of her children to see if they were all right. If any of them had been hurt, then so help her God...

"We need to call a ceasefire for everyone on the ground. That means PUC, Desian defense forces, civilians, militias, everyone. We need to coordinate with the ships in the sky, convince them that we still hold the ground, and that the mission is still viable."

"I thought you-" James began.

"Whether the mission is or is not *actually* viable isn't the point. If we can persuade them to hold off the bombardment, then we can buy time. Gather our forces."

"How do you propose to do that?" Vanessa asked.

"We have to convince them that there is another Light Wire facility and that we can reclaim it."

Silence stretched through the room and they could hear the sounds of people working in the docking bay nearby. The bunker was buried deep inside a rocky hill, shutting out most external noises, but the walls inside were thin and sound carried through the echoing corridors.

"So *lie* then," James said incredulously.

Hutchens nodded and as he did, Vanessa saw a look of fatigue flash over the colonel's face. He was good at hiding it but she was good at looking. The man had suffered a penetrating wound to the abdomen and while he seemed to be skating by on pain meds like so many others at the moment, she wondered how long that would sustain him.

"It's a tactical decision," Hutchens replied. "Right now, the most important thing is securing a base of operations. I believe that this isn't the only planet dealing with this." Vanessa saw 49 nod from his spot at the table. "So as far as I see it, there is no home to go back to at the moment. The greatest concentration of our forces is right here, so we need to secure this system, eliminate the hostile forces, and then push out. It's the only way."

*Ah*, Vanessa thought to herself. *There it is.*

Since the colonel had mediated the situation on the rooftop between her and Indigo Squad, she had wondered why he was being so reasonable. Now she had her answer.

"What are you talking about?" James said. "We need to get back to Lydia, regroup, and let these ingrates deal with their own problems. That's what they want after all, right? To take care of themselves?"

"Taking care of ourselves doesn't involve the PUC setting the planet on fire from *space,*" Vanessa snapped.

"Look," Hutchens interrupted. "There might not be a home to go back to. In fact, I'm almost certain there isn't. The Light Wire Network is connected to *all* of the star systems. So I'm almost certain they're under the same sort of attack. Right now, we're not just fighting for the PUC, we're fighting for *humanity.*"

Vanessa involuntarily gagged. She didn't know if the colonel actually knew how full of shit he was or if he was just doing what he was born to do. Climb the ladder.

Unfortunately, he was probably right.

"Do we know what the reach of the pulse wave is?" James asked. "How do we know the other planets here aren't just fine?"

"I can answer that," 49 said. "The Void energy piggybacked on the Light Wire, which means it can ride off of anything in that light spectrum, including stars. It was most powerful down here, which is why you heard the music, but chances are good it can jump from star to star until it's reached the edge of whatever star system it is in."

"And why should we listen to you?" James asked.

A beat of silence passed, then 49 leaned forward. "You should listen to me because I came from the Void. I have Void energy in me as well as energy from a Light Core. In many ways, I'm comprised of the mechanics that made this whole calamity possible."

"So what you're saying is, we should kill you?" James turned to Hutchens. "Right? We should kill him? I mean, he just said it himself. He's practically a walking Light Wire. Hell, we melt him into slag and maybe this whole thing stops."

"I am not a walking Light Wire," 49 said. "You use the wires as tools for spreading information. I am sentient. I have a will of my own."

"Those fucking *things* have a will of their own." James snapped. "Whatever made this happen has a will of its own."

"You're correct." 49 leaned back. "And we have chosen to act differently.

"So how are we going to do this?" Vanessa cut in. "How are we going to convince the PUC that we have another Light Wire?"

"Well, you should already know that by now, Vanessa," Hutchens replied. "After all, this is a military city. And as Head of Desia's defenses, you should certainly be aware of its assets." The colonel raised an eyebrow.

Vanessa's heart almost stopped beating in her chest.

Could he really be talking about what she thought he was? And if so, how did he know about it? Did the rest of the PUC know about it? Was her entire defensive strategy public knowledge?

"Yes, Vanessa. I'm talking about the Grade-5 Light Core you have hidden beneath the city."

"How do you know about that?" Vanessa asked the question bluntly.

"I didn't *know* about it until just now, but I suspected. You see: those pencil-pushers they have up there making the shots right now still don't know what you *are*."

"What I am?"

Hutchens nodded. He was pale and shaky but it was clear that this was giving him energy in spite of his wound. This was his life. His passion.

"You're not some enemy state with a matching fleet and army that's gonna duke it out over the skies of Desia. You're head of a defense fleet for a planet whose defenses are its own people. Your best strategy is guerrilla warfare. Fight and hide tactics. Sabotage. Kidnapping. Throwing Molotov cocktails through the living room windows of dictators. That kinda shit."

"So what does that have to do with Light Cores?"

Hutchens leaned in. "I know that your daughter, Byzantine Jackson, worked R&D in one of the first Light Core facilities. And ya know, when we first discovered who she was—who her *mother* was—I was confused. I mean, no Light Cores went missing when she was there. Seems kind of strange that a brilliant young mind such as herself wouldn't take *something* with her if she was going to succumb to—how do you say—-*separatist sentiments.*"

Hutchens smiled and shook his head. "You should have seen the chaos that unfolded in the ranks of the higher-ups when they figured out that the *daughter* of the Head of Defense for Desia had been working right under their noses in the Science and Research Division. She was already gone by then, of course. Probably spooked by the initial inquiries."

"She wanted to learn," Vanessa said flatly. "What kind of mother would I be for letting my position hold her back?"

"I looked to see if the outgoing manifests had been tampered with," Hutchens continued. "But as far as I could tell, nothing. I was stumped. I knew she had to take something, but I didn't know what."

"You sure have done your homework," Vanessa said with a crooked eyebrow.

"It's what they pay me for."

"Is it?"

Hutchens shrugged and spread his arms. "Okay, ya got me. They don't pay me for that. They pay me to send soldiers into killing fields until we stack up enough bodies that the enemy lays down arms out of pure exhaustion. That's what they pay me for. And ya know what?"

"What?"

"I *hate* it. I hate going in blind. I hate watching my men die pointlessly because the brass is too lazy to gather intelligence." He leaned back carefully. "So I decided I was done doing that. I was done doing what they told me and eventually, I started gathering my own intel. Building my own networks. I was an investigator before I was a commander and it's hard to pound that out of someone. But enough about me."

"Oh no. Do go on. I find this all very..." she threw a glance at James, "...*enlightening*."

"I know. I know. What I'm saying right now could be considered treasonous. But only if I fail. You see, the PUC only cares about two things: power and results. Everything else is just a means to an end. So if I pull this ground operation off, it doesn't matter *how* so long as I can make it happen."

"Yes, I'm quite aware of the PUC's utilitarian nature," Vanessa said. "Let's get a move on now."

"Right. So. Long story short: I had to check the *incoming* manifest for the Light Core facility that your daughter worked at and sure enough, someone had gone in and changed them. She covered her tracks pretty well, but not quite well enough. A part here and a part there. No one's gonna notice. But then after a while, you got yourself all the parts you need to build a Grade-5 Light Core. Once the incoming manifests were changed, all she had to do was take what she wanted and if they were to do an audit, nothing would seem amiss. The only manifests they'd really scrutinize would be the outgoing ones. Plus, little transfer errors happen all the time. It's inevitable. She just took advantage of it."

"Okay, okay," James interrupted. "Her daughter stole a Light Core. Who gives a fuck?"

"*We* give a fuck, James. We give a fuck because a Grade-5 Light Core is strong enough to power an entire anti-orbit weapons system."

"What?" James was incredulous. "Bullshit. If they had that kind of firepower, then why didn't they use it when they were attacked?"

"Because it still wouldn't have been enough," Hutchens said. "It would have been like three people fighting an army of a thousand rather than one. It would have greatly multiplied their chances of victory but not in any meaningful way. No, the whole reason they have it and are keeping it hidden is for when the fleet retreats and leaves just one or two ships in orbit. Then it's a fair fight. Then all of those militia groups you have hiding out can come and whoop our asses and drive us out. Then they pack up the Light Core and move it somewhere else so they can do the same thing the next time we come in. Maybe we leave more, but maybe they've also commandeered some more equipment in the process. Maybe even infiltrated our ranks. Every attack costs us a little bit more. And every successful defense allows them to grow. Not just in terms of physical assets but people as well. They get that propaganda machine running and feed every misdeed perpetrated by the PUC in their occupation out into the world and they can recruit ten times more effectively than if they were just filming cops violating rights on Lydia."

"I don't get it," James said again. "How is that a strategy? Lose so that you can *sorta* win later?"

"You'll never get it," Vanessa said plainly. "That's because you still don't understand your enemy. I knew that I could never get all of the militia groups to band together—not with all of their extremely stubborn ideologies. So I had to think of what to do *after* the PUC beat us in the initial battle. I have a very finite amount of resources in my position, so I had to devote them all to a battle I *could* win."

"This isn't the Pillon System's Capital," James said, comprehension finally dawning on his face. "This whole goddam planet is a *trap*. It's a *lure* for militia groups to kill PUC forces and divert attention away from the other 4 planets in the Pillon System."

"I think he's getting it," Hutchens said to Vanessa, but Vanessa wasn't smiling. Treating Desia as a trap for PUC forces had been a plan that she had worked to make a reality for years. It already had the highest concentration of armed militia members in the known universe. She had thought all the PUC high command were too dense to figure it out, and for all intents and purposes she had been right. But then this loudmouth commander had to come along…

"So here's the plan," Hutchens said. "I'll talk to high command and see if they can hold off for just a while longer. In the meantime, we get to the Light Core. We fire it up. And then we dial its energy output until it matches the signature of a Light Wire. The boys up top will undoubtedly do a scan, and that will buy us even more time."

"Then what?" James clearly wasn't on board with the plan.

"Then we convince them to help out with an isolated ground assault. They'll be air support as we systematically eliminate those things. They seem to be clustering, so we'll wipe them out pod-by-pod."

"Pfff," James leaned back and looked up at the ceiling. "That's easier said than done. What with that pulse wave hitting every couple of hours."

"I may have a solution for that," 49 chimed in. Everyone turned to look at him. "I believe I know how to make the pulse waves stop."

Everyone's eyebrows shot up around the room. Even the Marauders shifted in their armor.

"How?" Hutchens asked. "The waves seemed to be powered by something outside of this *realm*. Are you planning on going into the Void and politely asking it to stop?"

"Not exactly," 49 answered. "I plan on destroying the network it's using."

Now it was Hutchens' turn to look incredulous. "The network? What do you mean '*the network*' it's using?'"

"I'm talking about the Light Wire Network."

The android's words sunk into the room like a knife.

James turned to Hutchens. "He can't be serious, can he?"

"Why not?" Vanessa said.

"Why not?" James all but threw up his hands. "What are the brass gonna think when we ask them to give us time to boot up another Light Wire and then we just *destroy the whole fucking network*?"

"By the time they figure that out, we'll either have regained control of the planet or lost it to those things anyway," Hutchens said.

But James wasn't done. "And—*and* because without the regulated control of information, the entire People's Union Coalition would dissolve into chaos. Progress would grind to a halt. Dangerous rhetoric and misinformation would flourish. Citizens would *die*."

"They're *dying* now," Vanessa shot back.

"It is the *only* way," 49 said, obviously trying to squash the argument before it got out of hand. "There is no indication that the pulse waves will cease, and every time they hit, every person that has died since will succumb to it."

He let that thought sink in for a moment.

"There is a place—a sort of cerebrum for the Light Wire Network. If we can destroy it, then we can stop the signal. If we can stop the signal, then we might have a fighting chance. If we don't we'll just...drown."

"How do you know about this place?" James asked, skepticism plain on his expression.

"Because I've been listening to it."

"You what?"

"I've been listening to it. I have a Light Core-" He tapped his chest. "Right here. And I've been tracing the signal ever since it started. It's like a song. Only the first transmission was audible to the human ear, but it's matured in frequency since then and I've been listening to it the entire time.

Probing it. Following it. It's coming from somewhere in the Void. I've suspected for some time that there's some sort of central cortex connecting all of the Void Gates. Now that there's a sustained signal—and a strong one—I can finally begin to see the pathways."

"I literally didn't understand a word of that," James said flatly. "I'm pretty sure you're just speaking gibberish to try and get us on board with shutting down one of the central systems that connects and sustains our civilization."

"Hold on," interrupted Hutchens. "Did you say you have a *Light Core* inside of you?"

"I do. That's what I meant when I said I contained both Void energy and Light Core energy."

The colonel was stunned. He reached up and rubbed his chin. "Is it possible for you to amplify your output to match the signal frequency of a Light Wire? Could save us a trip."

"Unfortunately, no," 49 explained. "The Light Core in me is a Grade-3. It doesn't have enough *juice*, I guess you'd say."

"So. You'd be bringing down the entire Light Wire Network." Hutchens leaned back and stared at the ceiling. Vanessa could practically see the wheels turning. Weighing the odds. Pulling apart the fine matrix of possible repercussions.

"You can see why James and I might be skeptical."

"I can," Vanessa said. "It's what we've always wanted. This thing that's happening right now? It's what we've always been afraid of."

"What? A cosmic signal firing down from another dimension and transforming every dead human body into a living nightmare?" Hutchens cracked a grin.

"Well, not *exactly* that," Vanessa said. "But it's the

centralization of power we've been concerned about. The interconnectivity. We're all connected."

"We've always been connected," Hutchens retorted. "Since the beginning of time, our actions have always affected others."

"But there were boundaries. Borders. Geographical and spatial thresholds. It took time and that time allowed for adaptation. But the Light Wire? The whole PUC living in one instantaneous 'village' so to speak?" Vanessa spread her hands. "Look around you."

"No one could have predicted this," James spat.

"No one needed to predict *this*," Vanessa spat back. "You don't need to see the exact problem, just the potential for it. We were afraid something like this would happen. And it did. And now we're all fucked."

"Okay, I think it's about time we wrap things up," Hutchens cut in. "I'm in some serious need of a comfortable bed and a stiff shot of morphine. So we have a plan. I'll radio the brass. Indigo Squad will activate the Light Core beneath the city. The crew of—what's your ship's name again?"

"The Leopold," 49 answered.

"And the crew of the Leopold will destroy the Light Wire Network. Sounds solid to me."

"There's only one problem," Vanessa said.

"Oh yeah? And what would that be?" James asked.

Vanessa turned her eyes on them, mustering every ounce of gravity she could. "The entrance is beneath the hospital."

4

———

## CHATTER

"They're going into the hospital?" Raquel said, unbelieving. "From what I hear, that part of town is a damn hornet's nest."

The crew of the Leopold—minus Ritz, who was recovering somewhere in the medical ward—had gathered in a section of the bunker's living quarters that Byzzie had claimed for herself and the rest of her siblings. The space was dank. Bare concrete made up the floor, ceiling, and walls. The beds were sparsely blanketed, thin mattresses sitting on wireframes. The sound of siblings arguing bounced around the corners and blended into a constant drone in the background.

"Luckily, we won't be there to find out," Nadia said. Raquel thought she looked strangely out of place standing there in her Arc Suit as if she were wearing a pair of jeans and a t-shirt. The only piece that was removed was her helmet which was laying on one of the cots.

"Yeah, we'll be living it up in whatever hellscape 49 brings us to," King said, half to himself. He was laying face-up on one of the bunks, his eyes closed with the back of his right hand laying over his face.

"I don't think it's a hellscape," 49 replied. "I'm not sure what it is, but it's only peripherally connected to the Void. It's not a part of it."

"Cool," King replied, his voice flat. "And we're gonna go fuckin' nuke it or something?"

49 tilted his head, his gaze slipping to the floor. "Well, not exactly."

"What do you mean?" Raquel asked.

"I mean, the reality of it was a little too complicated to explain in that room," 49 said. "You should have seen it in there. No one trusted each other. They kept falling into circular arguments. And the Marauders just stood there silently the whole time. I honestly couldn't tell if they were even fucking awake."

"Whoa," King said, lifting his head off the pillow. "Did I just hear the bucket of bolts swear? He's turning into quite the teenager."

"Just trying it on," 49 said, smiling. "It wasn't very comfortable."

"It's not supposed to be." King held up a fist. "It's supposed to be *abrasive*."

"So what are we doing? Are we still shutting down the network?" Raquel asked, getting them back on track.

"We are. But it's going to be a little less destruction than I let on."

"So what then?" Nadia asked. "We gonna ask it nicely?"

"In a way."

"Uhhhhh," King groaned and let his head flop back.

"The place we're going to is called the Gaia Spine. And it's on Earth."

If he hadn't had everyone's attention, he sure had it now.

Byzzie, who was sitting and talking with a few of her younger sisters must have sensed the gravity from across the room because she excused herself from the conversation and came walking over.

"What's going on guys?" She looked exhausted. She had huge bags under bloodshot eyes and practically trembled as she stood. But her manner was calm. Cool. Not the manner of a person who just watched three of their siblings die a few hours ago.

Raquel made a mental note to check on her later.

"Oh, ya know," Kit said. "Just talking about how we're going to Earth."

Byzzie's eyebrows shot up.

"It's not exactly *on* Earth," 49 continued. "It *is* Earth. When the Earth was hit by the bolt of cosmic lightning during the Dislocation, the planet was physically shattered. But whatever energy comprised the bolt also imbued Earth with something. The pieces of the planet are still out there floating, and they're held somewhat together by a long gravitational cord. Earth was the epicenter of the Dislocation, and when it came apart, so did the universe. It's what created what would later become known as the Void Gates."

Byzzie's eyes looked like they were about to pop out of her head. "Whoa, whoa, whoa. You're saying that Earth is still out there. We can get to it. And the Dislocation is *in fact* the reason that the Void exists?"

49 shook his head. "The Void has always existed. But when the world came apart, there was something of a collision between this realm and the realm of the Void. They practically smashed into each other."

"Whoa..." Byzzie said, plopping down on one of the cots. "How do you know this?"

"I learned a lot of things when I was in the Void. I haven't been able to abstract and articulate it all yet though. It's an ongoing process."

"What did you mean when you said we'd essentially be *asking* to shut down the network?" Raquel said.

"There's someone there. Or something. On The Gaia Spine. I'm not sure who or what they are, but they're sentient and they seem to be a sort of guardian for the network."

"They guard the Light Wire Network?" Kit asked, confused. "Didn't we *make* the Light Wire Network?"

"We did not," 49 said. "Humans simply harnessed its power."

"Okay then," Raquel said, blowing out a long breath. "So we're going to Earth…"

Raquel had long thought about what Earth was like. Or at least what it had been like. Five years ago she had appeared on a distant planet called Lithoway with little else on it but a PUC medical facility. She had no memory. No name. Nothing. She simply washed up on the shore of a small river running through the otherwise arid landscape.

The funny thing was, she dreamt of Earth. Not when she slept, but whenever she passed through the Void. For most people, passing through a Void Gate was like walking from one room and into another, but not for her. For her, it was something more akin to being plunged into a cold black lake where someone else's past life had sunk to the bottom like an old ship.

The phenomenon was curious to her and the more times it happened the more desperately she wanted to unravel what it meant. The problem was, she was running out of time.

During a fight on board the Leopold a few weeks back,

she had cracked a live Light Core with the butt of a heavy pistol and then attempted to use it as a weapon. Things hadn't played out exactly like she had expected them to, but her Hail Mary had still won out in the end. Unbeknownst to her however, her bare exposure to the Light Core had affected the way her cells multiplied. In an awkward conversation with 49 before the attack on the medical warehouse, he had explained that she had contracted a form of cancer.

And the prognosis wasn't good.

So while she *wanted* to fly to Earth and talk to an ancient guardian and try to get it to save the world, she also felt the clock ticking. If she was ever going to find out where she had come from—or why she was there in the first place—then she would have to start looking soon or not at all.

"Hey," Nadia said quietly, pulling her back. Byzzie now seemed to be tenaciously grilling 49 for forbidden knowledge about the universe. Kit who had yet to say anything since they had sat down, was now inspecting his prosthetic. "You think she's okay?"

Raquel looked at the young woman. She seemed animated and lively but there was something underlying it. Something just barely out of sight.

"She's not okay," King said, startling the two of them. "Take it from someone who is frequently not okay."

"She hasn't talked about it at all," Nadia said. For being cold-hearted killing machines, both Nadia and Kit could be surprisingly perceptive when it came to people's emotions. Raquel often forgot that they were raised that way. As SEUs, the programming and training they underwent taught them to view their unit as a tribe and everyone who wasn't in that tribe could be eliminated as easily as squashing a bug. But as far as the inner group was concerned, they were incredibly in tune with each other's emotions.

"She will when she's ready," King said. "Some people need time to themselves before they can process grief. Being intellectually stimulated is how she's coping at the moment. It'll pass."

"Mmmm," Raquel thought about that. She felt helpless when it came to these sorts of things. Maybe that was normal, though. She gently changed the subject. "How's Ritz?"

"He's doing okay," King said. "He's got that silver lung on which assists with his breathing. He won't be doing jumping jacks anytime soon, but he also shouldn't slip into cardiac arrest either."

"Think he'll come with us?"

"I think he'd come with us even if he was unconscious. His body would appear on that ship like a damn apparition."

"Think he *should* come with us?" Nadia asked.

"Doesn't matter what I think," King said. "I'm done trying to control other people's destinies."

"Oh?" Raquel cracked a grin. "Does that mean no more impromptu bypasses that trip alarms and end in shootouts with a half-a-dozen combat synthetics?"

She immediately regretted the comment. The mission to which she was referring had also ended with them gunning down a room of PUC personnel. Most of which hadn't been armed.

"That's partly why, actually," King said with a sigh. He shook his head. "I'm not exactly ready to get into it. But if I hadn't done that, we may have been able to escape undetected. If we had been able to do that, then-"

"Then Hector wouldn't have died," Nadia finished the

sentence for him. Hector had been their old pilot who had died at the hands of a horrid nightmare creature not at all dissimilar from the Necrosarks. "You do your best. Sometimes you fuck up. People die. That's the game, man."

"Yeah well, I'm not sure it's a game I want to play anymore." King ran a hand over his bald head. "Ah shit, I'm just talking. I don't know what I want."

"If we hadn't taken that little detour through space," Raquel said, "Then we would have never picked up 49. And if we hadn't picked up 49, then we may not have been able to know what to do about the predicament we're currently in." She thought about that for a second. "Maybe Hector was a necessary sacrifice for the rest of humanity."

"Jesus, don't talk like that," King said, his face twisting. "We don't choose people to *sacrifice* for what we think the future should be."

"Don't we?" Nadia asked casually. "Isn't that what we do every time we blow a PUC ship out of the sky or eliminate one of their foot soldiers?"

King's face turned red, but he didn't say anything. Then when it looked like he was ready to come back with something, he was interrupted by a loud siren. Everyone's heads snapped up and Byzzie jumped to her feet.

"That's a proximity alarm," she said. "Someone's here."

"Or some*thing*," Nadia added, standing up. She reached down, grabbed her helmet, and then lowered it over her head. There was a snap as it locked into place. "Let's go stomp some bugs."

5

———

## ONSLAUGHT

There were three ways into the bunker. A docking port up top that the Leopold had barely managed to squeeze through, an escape tunnel that wound down and into the ground only to come up four miles later along the beach of one of the region's massive lakes, and a front entrance that—after a set of blast doors—opened up to a space about 100 meters wide and 350 meters long.

The port was sealed and obscured by vegetation and the escape tunnel had its own set of security doors that only opened from the inside. When the Necrosarks attacked, they threw themselves at the front entrance.

The entrance was barricaded by massive, electrified barbwire fences. The first wave hit the fences and was immediately thrown back in a shower of sparks and smoke. But not to be deterred, the ones behind them were already climbing over their thrashing bodies to hit the fence again.

"Can they get through that?" Ritz asked. At hearing the alarm, he had hobbled over to the nearest wheelchair and rolled himself to the communications center at the end of the hall. In the comm center, there was a large bank of monitors that Vanessa Jackson and Colonel Hutchens were currently hunched over. Ritz sat off to the side, 49 standing on his right.

"I don't know," Vanessa said uncertainly. They all watched as another wave of the monsters hurled themselves at the fence. The definition left something to be desired but Ritz was pretty sure he could see metal bands on the fence posts popping off as they bent and roiled with the attack.

"And what if they do?" Hutchens asked. His face was sweat-streaked and he wore a tight grimace. Ritz sympathized. Thankfully, he was at the peak of his pain medication while the colonel appeared to be reaching the bottom.

"If they get through," Vanessa explained, "the turret defenses will kick on."

"What kind of firepower?" Hutchens asked.

"Four fully-automated 30mm chain guns here, here, here, and here," she pointed out the positions on a map below the monitors. "There's also a minefield about thirty meters in. That should slow them down as well."

"Let's hope," Hutchens said.

Another wave of Necrosarks crashed into the fence and this time there was a loud groan of tearing steel. The structure held but ten seconds later the next wave hit and there was a loud electric snap as one of the posts buckled and the wire running along it tore. The creatures began to pour in.

"Here we go," 49 said. Ritz looked up at him and observed that he looked nervous, which was something he had never expected of a synth. It appeared as if the android was becoming more and more human by the day.

A muffled *brrrrrr* erupted from somewhere off-screen and six of the Necrosarks that were leading the charge folded and dropped in a cloud of black blood and fragmented exoskeleton. The ones behind it raced past their dead comrades and one of them was blown to pieces in a bright flash of light. A deep boom rolled through the bunker, followed by two more as the Necrosarks began hitting the mines.

"How much ammunition do those guns have?" 49 asked and both Hutchens and Vanessa turned to look at him.

"Enough," Vanessa said, turning back.

They watched in silence as more of the creatures died and more of them took their place. Another fifteen seconds passed and the attacking force had yet to relent. Just the opposite: it seemed as if they were throwing themselves forward with renewed effort.

"How much?" 49 repeated.

No one answered. Fed up, Ritz keyed his comm unit.

"Nadia, ready to go down there?"

"Aye, aye captain," Nadia replied. "I'm down here with the rest of Indigo Squad. Kit and the others are waiting at the set of doors behind us if they get through."

*If they get through.* Ritz felt his heart roll in his chest. Even if Kit and the others were able to finally halt the monsters' trespass inside, that would probably mean that Nadia would die with the rest of Indigo. He cast a quick prayer up to heaven. He didn't know if he believed in God anymore, but it was his friends standing there on the front lines if the turrets and the blast doors failed. His family. And as far as he was concerned, having his family's lives on the line was more of a foxhole than any other firefight he could remember.

He felt a hand on his shoulder and looked up to see 49.

"They'll be all right," the android said.

Ritz blew out a breath and tried to relax his jaw. He felt

his heart hammering and suddenly wished he wasn't on pain meds at the moment. He needed to be alert—needed his mind clear.

"One of the guns is dry," Vanessa said, her voice almost a rasp. The corpses of the Necrosarks were really beginning to pile up, making the whole image that much more confusing. Here and there, the bodies twitched and thrashed as they either died or were tugged at by a stray stream of bullets passing through them.

The mines had done well at incapacitating a number of them, but the dust and debris from the explosions made it look like the battle was taking place in a sandstorm. To tell the truth, the waves of monsters were far more intimidating now that they were so thoroughly obscured.

"Guns two and four are dry." Vanessa's shoulders were hunched and rigid as if she might snap the very console platform in half.

"I'm going out there," Ritz announced, spinning in his chair. He couldn't just sit here. Couldn't watch on some video screen as his crewmates died. He had to get out there. Had to do something.

A strong silver hand clamped back down on his shoulder.

"There's nothing you can do out there," 49 said firmly.

"Bullshit. I can hold a gun."

"Ritz. They got it."

"Do they, 49? Because quite frankly it doesn't look like it."

The distant buzzing noise of the last turret ceased and the room was filled with a deathly silence. The four of them remained completely still. Listening. Waiting.

"How thick are those blast doors?" Ritz asked quietly.

"Three feet," Vanessa answered. "It's reinforced steel. No way for them to get through."

"And the stone around it?"

"What do you mean?" But he could see the concern in her face.

"Those things were made for digging underground," Ritz said. "Just look at them."

Vanessa's eyes flicked back and forth over the monitors. Ritz could see the wheels turning in her head.

Hutchens ran a hand through his hair and turned around; Ritz was shocked at how pale he looked. His hands were trembling, his flesh sallow and sweaty. It looked like he could collapse at any moment.

"Nadia," Ritz said, refusing to wait any longer. "They're past the outer defenses and they could be coming in at any second. Watch the walls. The steel doors and reinforcements are thick but we think they might be coming in through the stone or concrete."

"Affirmative." Then, speaking to someone nearby: "Watch the walls, guys. Floors and ceilings too. No telling where these bastards will break through."

Ritz could see the Marauders in his mind's eye as they all spread out, aiming in different directions. He imagined one of the walls breaking apart as monsters spilled inside, filling the room with dust or maybe even collapsing it entirely. The bunker was supposed to be strong, but it was also old. Desia was an old planet with a lot of paranoid people that were more prone to dig a hole than run away. Who knew how long this bunker had been here.

"Wait!" Colonel Hutchens croaked, pointing at the screen.

But Ritz could already hear it. The sounds of heavy weapons fire. Men and women shouting. He wheeled himself closer to the monitors, his chest beginning to throb from the pressure. The stress.

Vanessa keyed her comms. "Nadia, you got people out there?"

"No ma'am," came Nadia's voice, crisp and clear over the comm line.

"King? Byzzie?"

Both King and Byzzie gave similar responses.

People were clearly visible onscreen now. They wore dark green camouflage and carried a variety of different weapons. Small ballistic carbines, light machine guns, and more than a few energy rifles.

Ritz watched as more and more appeared until there were about thirty on screen. They moved effectively and efficiently in tight groups. Firing in busts and in overlapping fields of fire, the line of newcomers pushed forward, driving the last of the Necrosarks back.

The monsters made one last dash forward. God they were fast. Ritz could hardly believe how fast they moved over open ground. None of them made it though. The last creature died with its legs thrashing as three soldiers poured bullets into its face and abdomen.

"Who are these people, Vanessa?" Hutchens asked, turning toward her.

"Unnnhhh," Ritz groaned, slouching in his wheelchair.

"What?" Hutchens turned around. A man had come up to one of the screens and was waving. He was heavily built with wide shoulders and a full beard. He had a compact automatic energy rifle slung over his shoulder and wore a large tactical belt with holstered sidearms on each side.

"An old acquaintance," Ritz said, his stomach feeling like it was about to sink through the bottom of the chair.

"Wesley Goff," Vanessa said, her voice neutral.

"Who is Wesley Goff?" 49 asked.

The room was quiet. Ritz tried to figure out how to answer him but Vanessa spoke first.

"Wesley Goff is the leader of the local militant faction."

"Which one?" Hutchens asked.

Vanessa sighed. "Kingsbane."

6

———

## PREPARATIONS

"Ritz!" Goff yelled as he walked through the door of the comm center. A few soldiers rushed in to pat him down for weapons. "Ya look like shit!"

"I feel like shit, Wesley."

"Well, you know the cure for that," the large man reached into his coat. The soldier patting him down hadn't gotten that high up yet and he suddenly backed up drawing his weapon, panic written all over his face.

"Whoa, whoa," Goff said, pulling his hand back out. "I'm just going for a flask, *officer*. Or is that illegal under the PUC now too?"

The soldier lowered his weapon, skepticism still writ large on his face.

"I think they frown on mixing alcohol and pain medication," Ritz said.

Goff came forward and slapped a hand down on his shoulder. "How ya been, brother?" His tone was lower now. Gentle almost.

Ritz just shrugged and gestured at his bandage. "Feels like I've got a twelve-pound bowling ball in my chest, but other than that..." He looked around the room. It was full of people but aside from Ritz, Goff, Vanessa, Hutchens, and 49, everyone seemed to belong to the PUC. Soldiers lounged here and there, chatting casually with their rifles slung over their shoulders. "...pretty fucking awful."

"Ha! You said it, not me!" Goff looked up at 49, who was standing off to the side. "And what's this thing?"

Ritz twisted in his chair. "That's 49. He's a sort of metal space god, I think."

49 lifted his hand and gave a casual wave.

Goff shrugged. "Fine, I don't need to know."

"So what's going on? What are you doing here? And more importantly: how'd you get so many people to follow you?"

"Well, Desia's a friendly place, ya know? I just started out with a small group of guys like when you and me were hittin' it. And eventually, it grew. No shortage of people looking to hit back at the PUC on this planet."

"Looks like they're hitting these fuckin' crab scorpions more than anything right now."

"Yeah, ain't that a bitch," Goff said. "I got more people with me than what you saw too. We came up from down south and have been hitting every bunker on the way to Glenhold. Most are empty, but we've found a few people hiding out. Once we've got enough, we're taking it to the bugs. Gonna take back the city."

"Yeah?" Ritz asked. "We've got an SEU squad heading in to take back the hospital."

"The hospital? What for?"

"Yeah, yeah, don't act like you don't know." Ritz looked over at Vanessa and made eye contact. She was chatting with Hutchens but looked far less laid back with all of the soldiers in the room. Hutchens looked up as well.

"Well, whatever you say. You gonna be there too? Been awhile since we've fought alongside each other. Be like old times."

"I'm not looking to repeat old times," Ritz said.

Goff sighed. "Look, man. We're going to be fighting these creatures. Maybe some PUC soldiers. It's not gonna be like—what I'm saying is: probably not going to be a lot of collateral damage? You know what I'm saying?"

Ritz mumbled something placating and politely pushed by him, heading for the door. He didn't need this right now. Not here. Not with everyone around. Without another word, he pushed himself forward, the wheelchair squeaking lightly as he made his way down the hall.

———

"Raquel," Nadia called from the other end of the armory. "Check this out."

Standing in full Marauder armor, Nadia made the pistol she held out to Raquel look like a toy.

Raquel walked over and accepted it butt-first. It looked a lot like her old pistol she had nicknamed the "Slugger." The Slugger had been a large .50 automatic handgun with a carved walnut grip. Unfortunately, it had been taken when PUC soldiers had forced them from Vanessa's home at gunpoint.

This pistol she was looking at now was similar but different in a few noticeable ways. It was the same make with a polished chrome finish and wooden handle, but instead of walnut, the wood inlay looked to be made of ebony. The most noticeable difference though was that instead of being an automatic, the pistol was a revolver in .480.

"Think this'll break my wrist?" Raquel asked hesitantly.

"Should be better than that fifty you had," Nadia replied. She was looking at one of the few Neural Rifles contained within the armory. The rifle was longer than the other Neural Rifles Raquel had seen, with a large magazine that fed into the butt of the gun and a small scope up top. "The frame might be heavier but you'll get used to that. Your wrists and arms will get stronger."

Raquel nodded, reassured. Then it occurred to her that she might not actually have the ability to get stronger. Not anymore.

She thought about her sickness. There was just so much that she didn't know about it. How long did she have? How fast would she decline? She had liked bigger handguns in the past because they were better at putting down combat synths, but they certainly wouldn't help her if she was too weak to hold them.

"Maybe not," she said, handing the pistol back. "Maybe something a little lighter."

"Okay." Nadia took the pistol and placed it back on its rack. She ran her armored fingers along a line of handguns and pulled out a smaller black polymer automatic. "This one's a 9-mil. But you see up here by the chamber-" she turned the pistol over to reveal a small green line, "-that means it has a built-in plasma accelerator with a diamond bore. These rounds can get up to 3,000 feet per second. 4,000 if you're using a 50-grain round."

Raquel took the gun and weighed it in her palm. "It's light. How's the recoil?"

"Most of the energy from the plasma acceleration is transferred directly to the bullet so there's very little recoil from that. You'll still have some kick-back from the powder but I'll see if I can find a muzzle brake for you. That should take care of it a *little* bit. Now, here's the cool part." Nadia knelt down to a small cabinet beneath the gun racks and pulled out a few boxes of ammunition. "These 50-grain shells don't use lead and have fragmenting petals that spread out on impact. The round isn't as heavy as your fifty, but the high velocity mixed with the fragmenting rounds should have almost as much stopping power."

"Will it stop a 'sark?" Raquel asked. "I was using a 10mm when we were attacked at the warehouse and it slowed it down but didn't kill it. I was hitting it in the eyes and everything and it just kept coming."

"Theoretically, yes. It's *super* expensive on the black market because it's still relatively new technology." Nadia looked down and gestured at the empty slot next to where she had gotten the pistol. "Yeah, see: of the five here, only one's already been snatched up. They probably didn't know what they were looking at. The tech here is meant to replicate the same ballistics of the Neural Rifles that Kit and I use. Now these bastards are tough, but we were able to put them down without a problem."

"Good." Raquel nodded. "Because I'm not sure I'll be lugging around rifles much longer."

"Why is that?" Even through the armor, Raquel saw Nadia's body language change. Tension. Concern.

Raquel explained what 49 had told her. About her disease and how she had contracted it through the Light Core.

"What's the prognosis?" Nadia asked.

Raquel just shrugged. "I haven't talked to him since. Everything I just told you is everything I know."

"Fucking Hell," Nadia said, leaning back.

The news seemed to visibly cripple Nadia and Raquel remembered that the SEU's training was different from that of most soldiers. When it came to the members of their unit they were taught to lean into their feelings. It made it harder to accomplish complicated objectives that required a calm demeanor and the compartmentalization of emotional responses, but if the bio-mechanical augmentations and Arc Suits made them tough as individual soldiers, their empathetic tribe-based training made them indestructible as a cohesive unit.

Kit and Nadia had undergone a rare form of transference, causing their tribal bonding to shift from that of their fellow SEU squad-mates to that of the Leopold crew after they had abandoned the PUC. While Kit had been the one to initiate their going AWOL, Nadia's bond with Kit had been so strong that it had overridden her own reluctance to leave. Kit had left based on a growing disillusionment with what they did. Nadia left because of her dedication to Kit.

The two Marauders had no romantic relationship as far as Raquel could tell. She wasn't even sure they were capable of such things. What she did know though was that they were fiercely loyal to each other and now to the rest of the crew of the Leopold.

Without warning, tears sprang to Raquel's eyes as she thought about Nadia's reaction. She had always felt a sort of outsider in the group as she was both the newest and had the least amount of connection to their overall mission and ethos. But it suddenly felt as if she was just as much family as the rest of the crew.

"You okay?" Nadia asked, hunching over.

"Yeah, I'm just—I guess I haven't really had a chance to process any of this yet. Not the sickness. Not anything." She reached up and wiped her face with the back of her sleeve.

Nadia wrapped a cold, metal arm around her and pulled her in gently. "I don't think any of us have."

Despite how impenetrable the Marauder armor seemed, Raquel felt herself relax against it. After a few seconds, she pulled away and looked around. "We should check on Byzzie. She lost family members today."

"Agreed. King's right, she needs space. But that doesn't mean we can't be there to offer support."

Raquel nodded and sniffed. She reached down and picked up the gun and ammunition off of the counter.

"I'll see if I can scrounge up a muzzle brake and a few extra mags for that thing," Nadia said. "You go find Byzzie."

It took Raquel roughly ten minutes of wandering to find Byzzie, King, and 49 in the hangar. In the far left of the room was a slot where the Leopold was docked. Four more spaces lay to the right, two of them occupied. One of the ships was another civilian class vessel similar to the Leopold, but it had so many rockets and machine guns added on it barely looked like it could fly. And to the right of that was a sleek stealth vessel made for deep space.

The clash of aesthetics between the two was jarring, a manifestation of the wide range of personal tastes held by the different militias and their members. The hangar was musty and cold, the smells of oil and wet concrete mixing together like a mechanic's shop that had fallen into disrepair. Considering the firepower and hardware they had built into the place, it was obvious that this bunker was nothing of the sort, but it felt nearly impossible to fully banish the feeling of being underground.

Raquel made to walk over to King, who was half-sitting/half-laying across a chair he must have pulled out of some storage closet. With a pen in one hand and a clipboard in the other, it looked like he was checking off items on a shipping manifest while Byzzie and 49 loaded them on. Before she made it across the hangar though, she heard a familiar gravelly voice call her name and she stopped and turned.

"Hold up," Hutchens said as he labored over to her. "I'm not quite fit to go running after you at the moment."

"Yeah, how're you doing?"

"Okay," he said, shrugging. "About as well as one can be after getting impaled by a giant scorpion from another dimension." He lifted his hand and gestured over to the others as they loaded the ship. "How about them?"

"Well..." Raquel observed how they moved—how King had his right leg laid out as if it were made of glass and could break at any moment. Byzzie, for her part, was hefting totes with her uninjured arm, likely given a sort of false confidence by whatever pain meds were in her system. Even 49 was moving slower than usual. The robes he was wearing obscured most of his body, but if one looked close enough, there was a visible hole in the front and back of them where he had been run-through by one of the Necrosarks.

"Looks like we all came out a little worse for wear except for you," Hutchens said, looking her over.

"I wish." The words came out a little harsher than Raquel had intended, showing too much of her fear. Her dread. Her grief.

"I got stabbed a few weeks back," she hastily added, pulling the neck of her shirt down to her shoulder, revealing a mostly-healed gash. "I had a little monster stab me through the shoulder before we got here. Not nearly as bad as Byzzie or King or you, but it still hurts."

"A little monster?" He asked.

"It was pretty horrid. Another Void creature. It was like a spider made of human ribs and finger bones."

"You seem to bring trouble with you wherever you go, don't you?"

"Do I?" She turned and looked at him. "I wasn't aware there was a place in this universe you couldn't find trouble."

"Not like this," he laughed, then grimaced, bending over slightly. After a moment he straightened up and spoke again. "Do you think it followed you?"

"Followed me? No, I don't think so. We took care of it the first time. This is something different."

"No," Hutchens corrected. "I'm not talking about following you from wherever you were a few weeks back. I'm talking about before. Before the Leopold. Before the medical facility. Before Lithoway."

The very air around Raquel seemed to freeze solid. She felt her skin prickle—heard the lure in Hutchens' voice.

*Lithoway. The medical facility.*

When Raquel had washed up on Lithoway five years ago, the only people living there had worked at a PUC medical facility close to where she had appeared. They had found her. Brought her to the small outpost. And had then proceeded to put her through a hellish litany of endless tests and experiments. There was no sense of time in the facility. She had possessed no memory or past. She had felt as if she was simply nothing. A baby in a grown woman's body, learning the vast depths of evil the world could inflict on someone one needle-prick at a time.

And in a jarring moment of recognition, a face swam up to meet her. A familiar face. It was brief. Momentary. Fragmented. But it was there.

Raquel turned her head to assess Hutchens. She could feel the emotions play across her entire body. Unbelief, followed by fear, followed by loathing.

He stepped back, raising a hand. "I didn't work there. I swear. I had no part in what they did to you."

Without thinking, Raquel drew the pistol she had just got from the armory and leveled it at the man's stomach. "You had no *part*?" The words felt like they were being squeezed out of her. "I *saw* you. You were there and you saw *me*. You saw me and the others and you did nothing."

"Who I was back then was an ugly person," he said, backing off.

"Back then? You landed on this planet with an invading army *yesterday*. I should put a ragged hole through you this very instant."

"I think I've already got one of those," he said gently, as if to remind her that he had taken a blow for her yesterday. One that could have killed her.

"So what, you think we're all good then? That you can just wipe everything away, just like that? Do you have any idea what they did to us there?"

"I know that the station was medical, but that's about-"

"One time they tested this drug on me for what must have been three months. They gave it to me four times a day. For the first hour, I would have the shakes so bad I'd often throw up. Then came the itching after that." She whipped up one of her sleeves, revealing old scars from gouges in her skin. "Then finally, I would break into a fever. I would sweat and hallucinate in my cell and then when it finally began to die down they would administer the next dose and it would start all over again. And those were just some of the symptoms. They were constantly tweaking the drug. Keeping that living Hell *fresh*."

Raquel rolled her sleeve back down. "That was just one of the things they did. I can go on if you'd like."

Hutchens looked like he was about to say something,

but instead, he stopped himself. Someone dropped a tool off somewhere in the hangar and the noise of it made Raquel realize how quiet it had gotten. She looked around to see everyone watching. 49 was striding over, his robe rustling in the awkward silence.

"There's nothing I can do to make that better," Hutchens finally said. "But the whole reason I tracked you down is that I'd like to try."

He began to reach into his pocket and Raquel jabbed the gun at him. Out of the corner of her eye, she saw a small cluster of PUC soldiers tense, the rifles they had slung over their shoulders slowly sliding into their hands. Hutchens slowed his movements, then held up a cautious hand to the soldiers, indicating for them to stand down.

"Be careful with this," he said, reaching down into a pocket inside his jacket. He pulled out a piece of office paper that had been folded three times.

Raquel took the paper from him and unfolded it. It was an incident report, dated almost five years ago. It was brief, summarizing her discovery along the riverbank and the following search for answers about how she had gotten there. A few people had floated the theory that she was a secret pet project of one of the bio-lab technicians that they had kept off of the books. When she had served her purpose, they had dumped her.

How surprised they must have been when she showed up sometime later with a trillion questions hanging around her.

The person who had written the report didn't subscribe to that theory, however. Apparently, one of the scientists had had the out-of-left-field idea that she could have been dropped in through the Void. There hadn't been any Void Gates or other cosmic anomalies in the area, but there had been cases of people disappearing into the Void and never reemerging or others who had shown up somewhere they shouldn't have.

So after some convincing, they had run an LSS or Light Signature Scan on her. An LSS was a unique string of coordinates within the universe that allowed the PUC to determine where a ship had come from if it traveled through a Void Gate without clearance and they had to retrace its origins. The coordinates themselves were how people used Tesla Arcs, and then eventually, Light Cores to navigate from gate to gate.

Raquel's eyes combed over the long string of numbers and letters at the bottom of the page over and over again. Everything else seemed to swim to the background. Hutchens. The room full of people. Her sickness. The conflict with the PUC and the Necrosarks. All of it.

This was it. The first step toward answers she had had in the last five years of her life. They had scanned her for a place of origin and she had given them a set of coordinates. She wanted to go there. She wanted to go there *now*.

"May I please take a look?" 49 asked softly. She jumped despite herself, unsure of how long he had been standing there. Her arm twitched as she tried to hand the piece of paper over but she found that she couldn't do it. So instead, he leaned over for a closer look. He blinked.

"Scanning the coordinates now." A few seconds crawled by and then he shook his head. "Unknown coordinates."

"What?" Raquel asked, feeling her heart begin to pound even harder than it had been. "Do it again. There must be some mistake."

"Unfortunately, there is no mistake," Hutchens said. "They discovered the same thing when you underwent the

LSS. The coordinates exist, but there's no known route to them. No Void Gate leads there."

"I have the number scanned into my memory core," 49 reassured her. "When this whole thing is over, we can search for it." Then, "I promise." He looked up at Hutchens. "Where did you get this?"

"I went to the facility on Lithoway to investigate a possible militant operative who had been leaking information. We found her, but in the course of the investigation I had to comb through all of their reports and communications over the previous decade." He reached into a compartment in his pants and pulled out a small tablet. "I never delete anything. So when I saw Raquel standing in the street yesterday, something pinged in my memory. It wasn't until today though that I was able to remember where I had seen her. I dove into my old files and came up with this."

The information should have been interesting to Raquel, but it all had a muffled sort of quality. Like hearing voices through a wall.

She had tasted the truth for a brief fraction of a second and then it had been ripped away from her again. *We can search for it*, 49 had said. But they couldn't, could they? Or at least, they probably *wouldn't*? Even if they made it through this conflict with the Necrosarks, who knew how long that would take? And she had a time limit. She could be dead by this time next month for all she knew.

"How long do I have?" She blurted. A question formed on Hutchens' face and 49 looked back and forth once between the two of them.

"It's hard to say for-" the android began.

"How long?" Raquel repeated, louder this time.

"Judging by the rate at which the cancer is spreading, a

year. Maybe two with treatment, which I think I might be able to administer myself."

One to two years. She would have thought that the news would be crushing, but to her surprise, it had a stabilizing effect. Considering how much had happened in the last day, it might be possible for something to break within that period.

At least now she had a timeframe to work within. She had the first beginnings of a plan.

## 7

## BELTS AND BLOCKADES

"Captain Holden, this is Colonel Hutchens, do you read?"

Vanessa watched Hutchens in the chair beside her take a deep breath and count to five. They had made contact with one of the captains earlier and convinced them to give them some time on the ground. Unfortunately, it sounded like they were having to deal with their own invasions onboard the ships, so now they were flipping through frequencies trying to get ahold of every ship captain they could and relay the same information.

Except nothing was getting through now.

"Captain Holden..." Hutchens tried again.

Nothing. The colonel put the comm unit down.

"Something's wrong," Vanessa said. "It keeps going down, not one channel but all of them."

"James mentioned the same thing," Hutchens said. "He's been trying to make contact with the SEU squad that's running point on the ground. He managed to tell them about the hospital but that was it. They got cut off."

"What do you think?" Vanessa asked. "Could one of your guys be jamming us?"

"I doubt it," Hutchens replied. "It's too inconsistent."

"The atmosphere on Desia is stormy. Communications cut out all the time here, but it's not like the signal gets fuzzy. More like it fails completely and all at once. I wonder if it has something to do with the Light Wire."

"The wire's destroyed," Hutchens said. "How could that be?"

"The wire is, but the signal clearly isn't." And that fact was certain. Not twenty minutes ago they had just been hit by their 9th pulse wave. "Maybe it's interfering with our communications as well."

The comm unit suddenly burped and a hard voice permeated with strain came over the airwaves, speaking fast. The signal was back up.

"This is Head of Fleet Command, Sydney Graham broadcasting on all channels. I'm running a foreign bio-organic scan on all orbiting vessels. All ship captains are to focus fire on any vessels with a foreign tissue rating over .7%. I repeat: any ships with a foreign tissue rating over .7% are to be fired upon until they are either grounded or completely des-"

The channel went dead. Vanessa turned to look at Hutchens. A sheen of sweat had just broken out on his forehead and she could practically see the wheels turning in his head. Trying to make sense of what they had just heard. Trying to strategize.

"They're firing on their own," Vanessa said, just in case he hadn't understood. "You know what that means."

Hutchens nodded solemnly. "The fleet is basically gone."

And it was, Vanessa thought. A fraction of the ships

overhead must have had Necrosark outbreaks onboard, but regardless of how large that percentage was, all but a few ships would be lost. As soon as they began opening fire on infected ships, it would turn into a free for all, leaving nothing but the highly skilled and the highly lucky. And while Vanessa wasn't quite sure what that meant for her yet, one thing she did know was that any minute now, there was going to be burning debris lighting up the skies of Desia.

"Our timeline just moved up. We need to get this thing underway," Vanessa said, standing up. "Right now."

Hutchens stood up as well. "We're not done loading up yet. I want to send some of my men to-"

"You have ten minutes," she said. "I'm going to go gather the crew of the Leopold and have them head out. This distraction is their best chance to make it through that blockade."

"We might not even need to worry about that," Hutchens said. "Hell, the whole fleet might be gone by the time this is done."

"But what if it's not? What if ten ships—or even five can regroup after the skirmish up there? They'll blast this place to smithereens. We can convince them not to if we fabricate the Light Wire signature. And if we don't, then we might have to blow them out of the sky. Either way, I want to be in control of that Light Core when the smoke clears."

"I'll find James," Hutchens said, his face hardening.

"Sounds good." The door to the center swished open and the two of them stepped hurriedly out into the halls, the sounds of their boots hitting the floor echoed off of the concrete walls. "I'll grab Goff and the rest of Kingsbane. You gather up your men and have them meet me in the hangar."

———

"Hope you're all loaded and ready to go," Vanessa said as she approached. King twisted toward her in his cot as Byzzie finished loading the last of the food supplies onto the Leopold.

"That time already?" He said.

"They're beginning to eat each other up there," Vanessa said curtly. "Byzzie, come here for a second."

King watched as Byzzie walked over to her mother. She had her arm in a sling and was visibly fatigued, but it was clear that she was doing better than he was, which made sense when he thought about it. The young woman had suffered muscular and tendon damage to her shoulder and it would probably be stiff for the rest of her life.

King on the other hand had sustained actual skeletal damage to his right femur and was gritting his teeth even in the deepest fathoms of his pain medication. Truth be told, he would pay someone handsomely to put him under for the next year or so just to avoid the painful recovery he knew was headed his way.

The pain in his leg was practically blinding him with what felt like bolts of lightning surging up into his abdomen. He could see 49, Ritz, and Raquel coming from across the hangar and figured that they'd be able to take care of the last of whatever supplies had to be loaded on. Or at least Raquel could. He doubted Ritz could lift a cloud of vapor out of a bowl in the state he was in.

It almost struck King to ask for some assistance with their mission. After all, 49 had made it sound like this was their one shot to get this under control and over half of the people embarking were so doped up on pain meds they probably couldn't be trusted to be *near* a gun let alone use it. Even Raquel and Kit were dealing with some ailments from their previous encounters aboard Mary's Burden a few weeks ago. They seemed to be managing better than the rest but it wasn't *nothing*. Kit had lost a hand for God's sake.

King began the slow and arduous ascent up the ramp when something caught his ear. It wasn't what was being said exactly—he was too far away to make out individual words—but how it was being said. Looking back over his shoulder he saw Byzzie and her mother deep in what seemed to be a private conversation.

The fact that they were even standing seemed totally outrageous to him. Vanessa had lost three children that day. Byzzie, three siblings. It was clear they were grieving in their own ways, but it wasn't exactly clear how.

When one of King's oldest friends, Hector, had died in the same fight where Raquel and Kit had been wounded, he had thrown himself into a long drunken stupor. It was destructive, selfish, and poisonous. Both emotionally and literally. He had isolated himself in his quarters and descended into his own personal Hell. When he pulled himself out a few weeks later with a hangover that felt like the end of the world, he had felt better. He wasn't sure if the booze and wallowing had been cathartic or if, by the time he was done, he felt too pathetic and degraded to continue down that path.

So he had sobered up, had a wonderful evening with his friends on the shore of a beautiful planet, and then once again been thrown back into the fray. He wasn't sure if he had moved on yet—the aches of loss were still deep and probably permanent—but being able to rebound with what essentially equated to his family had felt healing and cathartic.

As far as Byzzie was concerned, he had known her for only a few years and most of that time they had been in a constant struggle in both practical and theoretical domains.

Theoretical because of how idealistic she could be at times and practical because of how often their jobs overlapped. She was a tech wizard that seemed to make insane leaps and innovations when it came to improving the ship and the equipment they used, but it was King's job to conserve their resources and reign her in at times. They didn't have an endless bank account from which to spend money on the latest and greatest gadgets and at times the things she tried to build were simply too ambitious for the humble means of an outlaw vessel moving from job-to-job.

King watched from afar as Byzzie's brow creased and she seemed to be considering something. Then her back straightened and, to King's bewilderment, she began unbuckling her belt. Pulling the thick leather from her belt-loops, she removed a few small holsters and gadgets she had attached to it and handed it to her mother. Vanessa seemed hesitant at first, then finally reached out and took it. She undid her own belt and the two swapped. Once they were both buckled up, Vanessa put a firm hand on Byzzie's shoulder and leaned in for an embrace.

"That was fucking weird," King said to no one. Then he slowly hobbled to his feet, the springs of the cot screaming in agony. From there, he began making his way up the ramp and into the ship.

When he was halfway up, however, Vanessa called everyone's attention. People quickly formed up around her and she began to lay out her plan. He sighed heavily and plopped down on the cold steel beneath him. He sat there, half-listening, half-wishing someone would just come up behind him and knock him unconscious.

8

## GSW

The entire time Vanessa was speaking, Nadia's unease was creeping to the forefront of her mind. She registered the words the woman was saying, logging them in her memory for later. The thing that was slowly becoming more and more immediate however was the absence of Kit.

The last time she had seen him, they were all standing behind the blast doors waiting for the attacking Necrosarks to come barreling through. After that, they had split up. Nadia had met up with Raquel while Kit had gone to check in with Ritz. Ritz was now sitting in his wheelchair alongside Vanessa as she spoke. He looked exhausted and in pain. His skin was pale and a distinct tremor ran through his right arm. No Kit though.

Vanessa finished speaking and everyone began to get up. In an instant, Nadia was standing in front of the Captain.

"Have you seen Kit?" She let the urgency bleed through in her voice.

Ritz looked as if he had just been presented with some

complicated math equation, but slowly, he began to shake his head. "No, not since the ship."

"The *ship*?" Nadia turned and looked around the hangar. "Well, has anyone seen him?"

"What's this about?" Vanessa broke in, sensing the panic in Nadia's voice.

"Kit's missing." Saying the words made the whole thing more real and Nadia immediately sprang into action. "Vanessa, can you start asking if anyone's seen him?"

"Yeah sure, but how do you know he's missing? Maybe he's just off-" She shrugged her shoulders "-I don't know, taking a nap or something."

"We don't miss briefings," Nadia said, brushing the question off.

"It's true," Ritz added. "And if he had tried to get some rest, he'd have done it somewhere close to the action. These guys can fall asleep in ten seconds and be up and ready almost immediately."

"I'm going to check with the crew," Nadia said. She turned around and walked toward the others without waiting for a response.

The crew of the Leopold were all gathered around King, who looked as if he had just run a marathon and then had the shit beaten out of him.

"Kit's missing," Nadia declared. Everyone froze mid-conversation. "Raquel and 49, go check the armory. Byzzie, you come with me and we'll start sweeping the living quarters. And King..." She glanced the mechanic over. "Uh, you can stay here just in case he gets back."

King's eyes fluttered shut in relief.

"Okay people. Keep your comms on, keep your weapons close, and don't split up. If something happened to Kit, then it probably happened when he was isolated." She nodded at the group of them. "Stay safe."

The crew immediately paired off without question and set to their tasks.

THEY FOUND him in the generator room. It wasn't anyone from the Leopold who discovered him, but a few soldiers that Vanessa had pulled aside for the task. When Nadia burst through the door at a near sprint, the medics were already lifting him onto a gurney to shuttle him down the hall.

"What happened?" She demanded. "Is he alive?"

"He's alive," said one of the medics. He was a squat Asian man named Lee, according to his uniform. He moved quickly as he finished securing Kit, but when he spoke to Nadia, his voice took on a calm and soothing tone. "He suffered two GSWs to the abdomen. If I'm speaking plainly, he should be dead. The wounds are grievous, to say the least. Extreme bruising with burn marks around the edges. He appears to have been hit with some sort of advanced projectile."

*An advanced projectile. A Neural Rifle maybe?* Then Nadia thought about the empty slot next to the handgun she had picked out for Raquel. Stepping past the doctor, she made her way to the second body in the room.

A PUC soldier, by the looks of it. The man was splayed across the floor, the upper third of his body completely sliced apart, along with his right forearm. The severed hand was holding the new state-of-the-art pistol with the tell-tale green line running across the chamber.

"He lures Kit into the room," Nadia said to herself,

imagining the scene. "He says there's some problem. Something's breaking through the wall in the generator room and there's no time for backup." She stopped to think.

*Why wouldn't he key his comms unit and update us on the situation?*

Nadia made a mental note to check Kit to see if his comm unit was working.

"He steps inside and before he can ask anything, the man swings his gun across his chest and fires. Once. Twice." She mimed the motion with her fingers. "But Kit is already reacting—already igniting his Tesla Saber. He cuts the man in two, but by that point, it's too late. He falls to the ground."

Without warning, a deep pang of sadness rocked through Nadia. Kit had killed a man. The entire reason he had left the SEU program was that he was tired of killing people. Defending themselves against mindless monsters was one thing, but to Kit, human life was sacred. If he had gone so far as to kill his attacker, then he wasn't doing it in self-defense. He was doing so because he feared this man would target her next. Or maybe Ritz. Or Raquel.

Nadia straightened up as she finally accepted the inevitable.

Someone she had formed a temporary alliance with had turned on them and gunned down the closest thing she had to a brother. The attack had been planned. It had probably been done during one of the comms outages in a room where practically no one could hear them.

Vanessa had mentioned in her briefing that the comms kept failing. Was this why? Had they been taken down for this very purpose or had someone just seized the opportunity?

She wasn't sure, but when she put all of those pieces

together, the picture was an unnerving one. Someone was conspiring against them.

OUTSIDE THE OPERATING ROOM, Nadia stood ready in her Arc Suit while the extremely limited medical personnel rushed around her. She considered the possibility that they thought of her presence there as a threat—a promise of violence if they weren't able to save Kit.

She was fine with that.

Lee had been keeping her updated. Apparently Kit had internal bleeding, but not as much as one might expect. The anatomy of the SEUs was such that any sort of damage was localized to small areas in a way that was much more extreme than in normal humans. Sure, they could be stopped instantly by a bullet to the brain, heart, or spinal column, but anything else could be reasonably contained. What this meant, practically speaking, was that if a major artery was hit, blood was rerouted. If a vital organ was destroyed, one of the others nearby adapted to pick up the slack.

The hyper adaptability of the SEUs' bodies was due entirely to the alterations from the Tesla Arcs. Hundreds of reserves of energy lay nestled throughout their body affecting every cell and fiber nearby, each one ready to reproduce and mutate at a moment's notice. The cellular makeup of their bodies was a sort of antifragility so intense that—providing he made it through this—Kit's body would be ten times stronger and more adaptable than it had previously been.

There were drawbacks and limitations of course. First off, there was a threshold to how strong someone could get.

Second, if an SEU were to go an entire year without ample stressors to their bodies they would literally atrophy and die. The energy reserves would leak out. The cells would deteriorate and fail to replace themselves. In reality, the anatomy of an SEU was something of a mitigated cancer.

Nadia felt the muscles bunch in her back as she thought about cancer. About Raquel. About Kit laying inches from death in the room next to her. She felt tense. Anxious. It was the same kind of deathly impatience that occupied the quiet time before a massive conflict. The waiting.

She hated it.

Luckily, Byzzie rounded the corner at that very moment, followed by 49, Raquel, and Vanessa pushing Ritz in his wheelchair. "How is he?" Byzzie asked.

"He's fighting," Nadia said. "As you might expect." Then, with her voice lowered, "We need to talk."

Ritz nodded gravely. "I take it this wasn't an accident."

"Hardly. This was premeditated. He was lured, cut off, and attacked. He dispatched his attacker but I doubt he was working alone."

"Why do you say that?" Raquel asked.

"Because who the fuck is this guy?" She said. "I've never seen him before. Sounds like he's one of Hutchens' men, but who knows? Why would he try and kill a Marauder? Especially with those things out there. You would think everyone here would want any chance they could get."

"What are you thinking?" Ritz asked.

"I think someone put him up to it. Goff. Hutchens. I don't know. They either offered him something or threatened him."

"So what do we do?" Byzzie asked.

"We change our plan," 49 cut in. "We need to adapt in a way that they're not expecting."

"Any suggestions?" Nadia asked.

"Well, let's look at what they did," 49 said. "They tried to kill Kit, a Marauder. Our muscle, essentially. Perhaps they are trying to weaken us. So?"

"So we get stronger," Byzzie said. "We add more muscle."

"I can help with that," Vanessa said. "I don't have tons of people, but I can spare a couple soldiers at least."

"Good," Ritz said. "Someone you trust."

"I've got a few in mind. After this, I'll go round up Marcus and Samantha. They're solid." She stopped for a moment, thinking. "I'll also give you Amelia. She's older but an incredibly skilled nurse. You've got a lot of people hurting onboard. I think you'll need her." Then Vanessa nodded at Raquel. "You're the one who saved her. She had a concussion when she arrived at the warehouse we found you at. Was unconscious through most of the fighting."

"Her?" Raquel looked taken aback. "Look, I agree. We could use a nurse. But she was like...70."

"Yeah, she's getting up there, but don't be deceived. She's spent her whole life on her feet running back and forth from patient to patient. She helped me out a few years back when I took a plasma bolt to the thigh in that nightmarish conflict with those human traffickers." She glanced over at Byzzie who nodded in confirmation.

"That should be fine," Ritz said, and Nadia figured he must have been somewhat relieved to be getting a nurse onboard considering his injury. "Just make sure you have someone here you trust as well. Kit's staying, so we'll also need someone to watch him."

"Whoa," Nadia said. "What do you mean Kit's staying? This is the worst place he can possibly be. What if they try again?"

Ritz shook his head. "He'll slow us down. Divert our

attention. Plus, he's in rough shape and we need to leave *now*. We don't have the equipment to keep him stabilized onboard."

"No," Nadia was shaking her head. "I think that's what they want. Guys, this has the whiff of revenge to it. I don't think it's tactical. I think it's Indigo getting back at us."

"Nadia," Ritz said. "We *can't* have him on board. We don't have the equipment. He'll die."

"Then I'm staying here," Nadia declared.

"Out of the question." Ritz seemed to muster all the authority he could. "Look, I know what Kit means to you. But not only are you the one that can swing the biggest fist, so to speak, but you're the only one of us that's not injured or otherwise occupied. Look around. Raquel's still recovering from the fight aboard the Mary. 49 will be piloting the ship. I've got a mechanical lung," he gestured at the silver contraption over his chest. "Byzzie's shoulder is fucked up and King can barely remain conscious." He looked her hard in the eyes. "If it comes down to a fight, we *need* you."

Nadia didn't like it. In fact, she hated it. But she understood. Kit had to stay here and she had to leave. It was their only shot but it felt wrong. It felt like betrayal.

"He better be here when I get back," she said, relenting. "If he's not, someone's going to pay." She turned to Vanessa. "You keep a guard on him 24/7, got it? And not just some asshole. Someone you trust with your life."

Vanessa nodded. "He'll be safe here." Then, "You all need to go. Time is running out. Indigo Squad is already away. We can contain the PUC threat but I'm not sure how many more pulse waves we can take. People are dying all over this planet right now and eventually, those things are going to come calling. We need to stop this *now*."

"You heard the lady," Ritz said, lifting his hand. He twirled his finger in the air, gesturing to be turned around. "Let's hit it."

## 9

## FIRE IN THE SKY

The Leopold bucked as it shot upward into the sky. Byzzie was back in the gunner's seat with 49 at her side. Behind them sat Ritz in the Captain's chair with Nadia sitting to his right, just in case he passed out. The rest of the crew, including the three additional people Vanessa had assigned them, were all back in their quarters, watching the ship's progress from their viewscreens.

The "silver lung" that Ritz was wearing on the left side of his abdomen was supposed to keep his chest from caving in on itself. He had taken an energy bolt down on Desia and had only managed to survive due to some quick thinking from King. He had then been dragged unconscious through the streets of Glenhold and at least two firefights, depending on how you counted them. All things considered, the fact that he was even conscious was a miracle.

He supposed he owed that to the complicated cocktail of drugs in his system. He felt both cranked and exhausted at the same time, rather than one or the other, and the very act of existing felt vaguely tenuous.

"We got bogies," Byzzie said, and as she did the ballistics

system that ran along the side of the ship thrummed to life as two rows of swiveling barrels began spewing lead.

"What are they?" Ritz asked.

"Some sort of flying Necrosark," Nadia answered. She leaned in to peer at the screen in front of her. "They look different than the ones Kit and I encountered though. They look bigger."

"Great," Ritz said. "Byzzie, are they dropping?"

"Sort of," Byzzie answered. She was jerking the firing joystick back and forth as she tried to secure a lock. "I know I've hit a few, but they're moving so fast it's hard to tell. Maybe if 49 would keep the ship still for one damn second."

"Can't," the android answered from the pilot's side. "I don't how dangerous these things were when you encountered them Nadia, but I don't think they would do this hull any favors if they got ahold of it."

"They did some damage," Nadia replied. "But as I said, they were smaller. With these things, I'm not sure."

"They may have grown," 49 said as he dipped and dove through the attacking creatures. "When you faced them before, they'd just been born a few hours earlier. It seems like the Necrosarks on the ground have an incredibly advanced metabolism, causing them to grow at a massive rate when they eat. It's possible that these things are more developed."

Ritz caught a glimpse of one of the horrid creatures through the viewport as a ballistic round chopped the side of its head off. It thrashed in the air and was quickly lost behind them as they rocketed past, but the fact that it didn't instantly go limp at having its head destroyed was unnerving.

"So what, they can just grow forever?" he asked.

"Unsure," 49 said. "I doubt it though. They probably just

eat and grow until they reach a mature state. Who knows what that looks like though. You have to remember, we're fighting an enemy that we have yet to understand. We don't know how they eat, breed, communicate. Any of it. We don't even know how smart they are."

"They didn't seem too smart as they were running into a face full of my bullets," Nadia said.

"True, but again: those were probably comparable to children. I think there's an intelligence behind these things that we haven't seen yet."

"Well, I'm seeing *something* up here," Byzzie said.

The ship rocked as a huge, spindly body slammed into the viewport. From a distance, the things looked like bugs, but now that he saw it up close, Ritz felt his stomach twist. The monster's numerous eyes were shiny and black, but they shone with an intensity he had never seen in any sort of animal. He felt them stabbing into the enclosed space. Hungry. Desperate. Almost tortured.

Ritz had seen the look only once before. In a prison camp set up by Kingsbane to interrogate PUC officials, he had met a man who had literally had the humanity tortured out of him. The look in his eyes was loathsome, his entire self reduced to a speechless sack tied together by a loose network of uncoordinated reflexes. He had simply become a product of the environment.

That's what this thing looked like, and just before 49 spun and rolled the ship, managing to hurl the monster off of the viewport, Ritz truly realized that what they were fighting wasn't some sort of dangerous animal. They were fighting something akin to lost souls. Or demons.

"We're almost there," Byzzie yelled. The racket on the ship had become immense from the combination of gunfire, atmosphere, and the banging of the huge Necrosarks as they careened off of the side.

Just before the Leopold broke atmo, a massive gout of flame blossomed in the sky, the sound of thunder rolling across the ship.

"What the fuck was that?" Byzzie said.

"A ship," 49 answered. "They must still be duking it out up there."

And Ritz saw that he was correct, for at that very moment, the atmosphere dissipated in front of them to reveal utter chaos. The debris of the destroyed fleet was so thick it looked as if the asteroid belt that surrounded the planet had expanded to ten times its normal size. Here and there, ships were still ducking and weaving in slow strafing patterns as they burned each other out of the sky. Another vessel detonated, this one even closer, and when Ritz squinted he saw dozens of tiny specs wriggling against the black blanket of space like a sea of dancing stars.

They were bodies. PUC personnel that had been vented into the vacuum of space to suffocate and die.

"Get us the fuck out of here," Ritz said. "That's an order."

———

"Orbital imaging shows most of the fleet overhead has been neutralized," Hutchens said in a cold voice. He shook his head. "I hate to say it, but this never would have happened if Seamus Clark was up there. Graham's an asshole. A panicky bureaucrat that wormed his way into that position by kissing ass and making promises he'll never keep."

"Yeah, well," Vanessa said, her voice just as cold. "They can fucking burn."

Hutchens seemed to absorb that for a moment.

Goff had left momentarily to grab a cup of coffee, leaving the two of them alone in the comms center. Vanessa felt the tension build in the silence but she didn't care. And she let him know that.

"I'm not going to apologize. That's the way it is." She said it like a fact.

"We're on the same side here," Hutchens implored. "I think it's important we overcome what happened yesterday so we can work together towards a common purpose. I see you as an ally right now."

"Look," Vanessa said. "I get what you're saying and I agree with you. It's important that we work together for the time being, but that doesn't make things right."

"It's hard for me to understand what you're going through," Hutchens said, lowering his voice. "You lost children yesterday. You're hurting. But we didn't kill them. Those things did."

"Let me put it this way: if a cop busts down my door and lets a snake into my house in the process, I'll kill the snake but I'll blame the cop. You get me?"

Hutchens exhaled. "I get you. But we have a unique chance here to overcome all of that. The PUC fleet is gone. The capital is probably burning. This is our opportunity to start again. To use the building blocks of what's been broken to build something new. Something better. I think with our combined influence, we can build a system that works *for* the people. It'll be a tough fight, but if we do this right, then every living person can experience safety and security in a way that they never could under the PUC."

"Safety and security." Vanessa said the words without any intonation.

Hutchens held up his hands. "That's not what I meant. I

mean we can build a system where people are free. Where they can thrive. And it can all start *right here*."

Vanessa wanted to go further, to break apart whatever vision of the future this man sitting next to her saw, but at that very moment the door to the center slammed open as Goff trundled in. He was carrying a tray with three cups of coffee on it, steam rising into the air.

"They in yet?" Goff asked, referring to Indigo Squad. He plopped down heavily into the chair and passed out the coffee.

"Not yet," Vanessa said, looking at the screen. "They're close though, about one klick away. No action so far"

"Have you been able to hail them?"

When Vanessa had entered the comm center after talking with the crew of the Leopold, Hutchens had explained that for whatever reason, they couldn't make audible contact with Indigo. All of their helmet cams were working though except for James's. Judging by the strength of the signal, Indigo had still been getting audio though. And if the signal was being blocked, they wouldn't be getting anything at all.

It struck Vanessa that Indigo Squad might actually be able to hear them, but had simply chosen not to respond. James's helmet cam was off, but not busted, which gave her the impression that he had turned it off voluntarily. All of that added up to the possibility that Indigo had formed some alternative plan and were currently putting it in motion. Add that to Hutchens' remarks about creating a new "system" and the attempt on Kit's life and Vanessa was beginning to feel more than a little paranoid.

She reached down for the hundredth time and checked her sidearm. Still there. Loaded. Lethal. If anything happened, she wouldn't be going down without a fight.

"Not yet," Hutchens said. "We've been trying every five minutes."

"Weird. What about bugs? Any action along the way?"

"Surprisingly, no." Hutchens took a sip of the coffee, grimaced, and set it down. "No signs of life. Human or otherwise. It's a ghost town out there. Only bugs we've seen have been in the air when the Leopold left."

"Probably all died when Indigo took the warehouse." Goff let out a deep gut laugh. "Maybe Desia is ours again and we don't even know it yet."

"Doubtful," Vanessa said. "It's more likely that they're all holed up somewhere. Probably, the hospital. Which is unfortunate for us."

Goff laughed again. "Unfortunate for Indigo, you mean. I couldn't give any less of a shit about 'em, to tell the truth."

"Am I the only one here that understands the situation?" Hutchens said irritably. "We *need* to succeed at this or any ships left up there are going to turn this planet into a hunk of glass."

"No," said a voice behind them. "You're not the only one."

Everyone spun to see James standing in full SEU armor behind them.

"James," Hutchens said. He spun to look at the screens and then back. "Why aren't you with your squad."

The massive figure stood silently in the doorway, not answering.

"This is me asking as your commanding officer, soldier." Hutchens' voice was glacier cold. "Why aren't you with your squad?"

James took a small step forward, his hand drifting down to hover over the large pistol strapped to his thigh. Vanessa felt herself tense, her hand moving toward her own involuntarily. Could she beat an enhanced human's reflexes? Would a bullet from her weapon even penetrate that armor? She felt small droplets of sweat spring out on her forehead. And out of the corner of her eye, she saw Goff's hand resting on the butt of his own weapon.

"I wanted to make sure we had somewhere to come back to," James said. "What with the attempted killing of Kit, I figure we're pretty vulnerable here." He tilted his head slightly. "From inside and out."

"That's all well and fine," Hutchens grated. "But what about your team? I think they might need their captain right about now, don't you?"

"I have no doubt that they can handle it," James said. "And I figured this was too important to pass up. It's clear that someone here is maneuvering behind our backs, so I figured our best shot was to do something unexpected. Now if someone tries something while the muscle is away, they'll get a little more than they were bargaining for."

"My soldiers aren't exactly pushovers," Goff said.

"I'm not even going to respond to that," James said. Even though Vanessa couldn't see the man's features through his faceplate, she could hear the snarl on his lips. If there was anything Surgical Equalizing Units hated it was militias, and Kingsbane was one of the biggest.

The corner of Goff's own mouth twitched as he suppressed a smile and Vanessa knew why. The heavy revolver the man wore on his hip was one he had made himself for the express purpose of bringing down SEUs and combat synths. Similar to the rounds that had put Kit out of commission, the bullets fired from that gun were plasma-accelerated. The revolver's caliber on the other hand was far larger than that of the standard 9mm Kit had been hit with.

For the briefest of seconds, the thought that Goff was

behind the attempt on Kit's life flashed through Vanessa's mind. Was that possible? She didn't want to consider it but she had to. The would-be killer had used plasma-accelerated rounds. She knew Goff and his men hated SEUs with a burning passion, but did that extend all the way to defectors?

Kingsbane was an extremist group and it was possible—no, probable that a few of them were extreme enough to hate Kit just for what he was, despite whatever actions he had taken to correct his path.

Feeling as if she suddenly had no friends, Vanessa wanted to shrink and disappear. She resisted the urge, however, and stood up.

"James," she said. "Your team is entering the hot zone as we speak. So either pull up a seat and sit down or get out of the room. I won't run an operation with you breathing down my neck, got it?"

James snorted. "Yes, ma'am."

"And tell them to start responding to our hails," Hutchens added. "We can't run this op without communicating."

James's posture said that he heartily disagreed, but he sat down at one of the consoles anyway and turned it on. Within seconds, the screen had linked up and he was watching his squadmates walk through the lobby of the hospital.

"Indigo, this is James. Do you read?"

"Affirmative," said a female's voice. The name on her Heads Up Display read, "Charlene."

"I'm at the comms center with Hutchens and Jackson. We're monitoring."

The view on Charlene's small helmet cam jerked up and down in acknowledgment.

"What's it look like in there?" James asked. They could clearly see the inside of the lobby through the cams but Vanessa knew there was a distinct difference between seeing something through a video feed and experiencing it.

"Signs of a struggle," Charlene said. "No movement though. Looks like the action has moved on." She panned over the interior of the hospital's lobby, revealing numerous flipped waiting room chairs and end tables. Several panes of glass were broken and the small pebbles littered the ground along with an assortment of other refuse. There was also the occasional dark patch on the floor but through the cams, it was hard to tell if it was blood or just deep pools of shadow.

"The Light Core is in the 4th basement level," Vanessa explained. "There's no elevator access so you'll have to take the stairs. The door to the nearest staircase should be around your first corner to the west and the first door down the hall."

The three helmet cams each covered a different section of the large, devastated room but it was clear they were all grouped together, back to back. Vanessa marveled at how the Arc Suit technology turned what would have been a pretty terrifying setting into a clearly defined battle scenario. The neural networks that tied their armor into their very brains illuminated their Neural Rifles' reticles as they moved over the environment and used a soft night vision system to enunciate the hard lines of structures in the dark.

"Indigo Squad advancing," Charlene said. And with that, the three first-person views pressed forward into the abandoned hospital.

**10**

---

# CHOICE

The violent disintegration of the PUC fleet provided all the cover the Leopold could have ever asked for to mask their escape. Once they broke through the atmosphere, the bugs fell away leaving the plummeting vessels as their only real obstacle. Navigating the field of wreckage had been a little touch and go as the broken ships came apart around them, but they soon made it through and the Void Gate on the other side yawned open at them, empty and unguarded.

"Putting in coordinates now," 49 said.

Byzzie checked and double-checked her screen. "Those don't look like any coordinates I've ever seen."

"I suspect that this *place* doesn't look like anything you've ever seen," 49 said. And before Byzzie could reply, they were through.

---

RAQUEL WAS DROWNING. Black water seemed to be forcing its way into her mouth like a million clammy fingers, trying to pry and press their way inside of her. She could feel the nothingness around her. The stone-hard black of the Void, rushing over her naked skin. Her body heat a flickering candle against the relentless hammer of the wind at night, threatening to gutter out any second. Holding out against hope. Against sense.

Black stars blossomed in her head like the spread of some deadly fungus. Every memory comprising the thin existence of Raquel Fisher bent and dissolved. Her skin separated and sloughed away like the flesh of a rotten fish. And soon, there was nothing left but the quiet water, lapping at the unobserved bottom of existence like a persistent tongue.


RED-HOT PAIN SURGED through Raquel's chest as she gasped so hard and so deep that every muscle in her body groaned with the force of it. The stale compartment air of the ship pounded into her so hard she was afraid she might literally pop. Unable to control herself, she gasped again and again, gulping down huge mouthfuls of oxygen. The world shifted slightly, she leaned to the side, and then proceeded to heave her guts out onto the cool metallic floor of the Leopold.

She had expected this and planned on throwing up into the garbage can bolted to the floor at the end of her bunk. But the experience had been far more turbulent than she had predicted and as the fog from her head slowly cleared, she realized that she had rolled almost to the other side of the room.

For some reason, Raquel had a violent reaction to Void traveling. As far as she could tell, no one she had ever met reacted the same way she did, but it had occurred so consistently now that she expected it.

In the past, she saw something like a dream in her head in that brief state of unconsciousness where she passed through the Void. The sun-kissed hillsides of summer. A gently sloping mountain with a rushing river crawling toward the ocean. A woman in a purple dress, sitting at a wooden picnic table with the faces of family and loved ones swimming around her.

That woman was Raquel. Or at least, she felt it was. There was no way to be sure.

Ripping a sheet off of her bunk, Raquel quickly used it to clean up the mess she had made. When she was finished, she balled it up and stuffed it down into the garbage can she had intended on using in the first place.

She then proceeded to the ship's wash area where she rinsed her mouth out, spat, and drank three large mouthfuls of water. The acrid taste of bile still lingered in her mouth but she'd have to get over it and just make sure she didn't get too close to anyone.

As if that mattered at the moment.

Refusing to let every problem in the galaxy swarm her all at once as they tended to do, she focused on making her way out of the wash area, down the hall, and onto the bridge where everyone but King and the newbies had gathered.

When the door to the bridge slid away and she stepped up next to the Captain, Raquel's breath caught in her throat. The viewport in front of her displayed space like she had never seen it before. It seemed as if every color of the spectrum was dancing around them, bending and flowing into each other in a convalescence of light that brought to mind something verging on magical.

"What is this?" she asked, astonished.

"When the Dislocation occurred and humanity was flung across the stars," 49 said. "A thousand planes of existence were hurled together, cleaved in two, or torn apart. In our case, it was torn apart. What you see before you are like radio signals from other planes. Like the lights of stars, some still continue to exist while others do not. This is where, for a single instant in time, a thousand parallel lines suddenly and inexplicably touched."

"Looks like a slick of oil on pavement," Nadia said. Her head was tilted forward and she seemed completely uninterested in the spectacle passing before her. She had a standard metal knife in her hand and was tapping it lightly on the deck of the ship.

*Tick, tick, tick.*

The concept was difficult for Raquel to understand but the visual had a way of communicating it in a way that words never could. To her, this felt like the center of everything. Ground zero of the Dislocation.

The Dislocation had occurred over three centuries ago when a bolt of cosmic lightning had hit the planet and scattered humanity amongst the stars. People woke up to find themselves on hostile planets, some disconnected forever from their families. Some didn't wake up at all.

"49," Raquel slowly asked, "What *was* the Dislocation? What caused it?"

"Nothing caused it," Ritz said irritably. "Sometimes shit just happens."

"Shit like, the world tears itself apart?" Raquel asked.

"Yeah, actually. I don't know if you've noticed, but it seems like that happens all the damn time." Ritz grimaced and Raquel thought she saw sweat break out on his forehead. She suddenly felt stupid for asking such questions while her captain was in so much pain, and clearly just wanted to focus on the task at hand.

"Just look at what happened on Desia," he continued. "A

fucking army dropped out of the sky, hooked up their little machine, and accidentally tugged an assload of monsters out of god-knows-where. There's no *why*. No reason for it. Things just happen."

"It's hard to say," 49 said, not disagreeing with Ritz but not agreeing with him either. "It does feel like things just happen though, doesn't it?"

Byzzie spun around in her seat. "I'm pretty sure you said you were Catholic or some shit yesterday, right? Shouldn't you be busting out the 'all things happen for a reason' mumbo jumbo?"

"Wesleyan, actually," 49 said. "And not exactly. I believe that everything can be redeemed towards a greater purpose. I believe that is what we are called to do as living beings on this plane of existence: to redeem the broken world. I believe that in doing so we embody the crucified son of God and God works through us to accomplish his task. However, I make no claim as to knowing the degree to which events are dictated by a guiding hand."

"So God could do things but he doesn't?" Byzzie asked, raising her eyebrows.

49 titled his head. "Nadia, you love Kit, correct?"

Nadia stopped tapping the knife against the deck. "Not in the way you might think, but yes. I guess you could say that."

"Now imagine he hated you—that he couldn't stand to be near you."

"What are you getting at, 49?" Ritz interrupted.

"Yeah," Nadia said, her voice quietly lethal. "What are you getting at?"

"Bear with me, please." The android held up a silver hand. "Nadia, given that scenario—that he hated you but you still loved him—would you *make* him love you?"

"What kind of question is that?" She asked. "You can't make someone love someone else."

"But suppose you could. Suppose, with a snap of a finger, you could change him and make him love you. Would you?"

Nadia shifted uncomfortably in her armor.

"Of course not," 49 answered for her. "Because to force someone to love you would be to negate the key aspect of love: choice."

"That's all well and good," Byzzie interjected. "But what does this have to do with anything?"

"The element of choice is a key ingredient to creation —at least, a creation where love is possible. And for choice to be present, the possibility for bad or wrong choices must exist. Therefore, even in a world with an all-powerful God watching over us, evil still exists. It exists because it must exist. If it didn't then neither would love, grace, or anything else in this world worth fighting for. Creation exists between polarities. That is simply the truth."

"I think I'm done with this conversation," Byzzie said, turning around to look back at the screen. "I don't need the robot who killed literally hundreds of people, including one of my friends, to lecture me on love and God."

What Byzzie was saying was true, Raquel thought to herself as she listened to the conversation. When they had first stumbled upon 49, he was a murderous entity bent on their subjugation, degradation, and ultimately: their elimination. Using something not too dissimilar from the pulse wave that created the Necrosarks, 49 had wielded the *Song of Infinite Communion*. Raquel remembered the piece of music—if one could call it that—as being both haunting and seductive. It offered death but it also offered peace. And at that point in Raquel's life—which had not been *that* long ago—she had almost fallen under its spell.

The people aboard the ship before them who *had* submitted to the *Song of Infinite Communion* had turned into mindless shambling monsters. Their bodies rearranged in a grotesque parody of human anatomy, the creatures had been a frightening and almost unstoppable force. It wasn't until, while wielding the very Light Core that had given her her terminal illness, Raquel had disabled and altered 49 into what he was today: a new creation. Kind where he was once cruel and gentle where he had been rough and violent, the android seemed to have gone down some path of spiritual seeking. The ship they had found him on *had* been a missionary vessel after all, and its data banks along with his crew had held vast knowledge and theological insights into the mysteries of creation.

"Do you believe in Heaven then?" Raquel asked 49. She wanted to shift the subject and was genuinely interested in his answer.

"I do," he said. It was clear that he wanted to say more but he stopped himself.

Raquel waited. Then, looking around the bridge, she noticed everyone turned away from her. Apparently, even in a crisis situation, news traveled fast. She understood.

The dying woman asking about life after death. Clinging to some hope, however irrational it might be. No one wanted to stomp on that. What was more, it seemed that 49 didn't even want to expound on his thoughts on the matter. After all, they were no longer talking about abstract ideas, they were in dangerous territory where theorizing out loud might potentially have some great impact on what she thought and believed moving forward.

Raquel wasn't about to put up with it. If she had to walk

through the rest of her life with people censoring themselves in front of her just to make her feel more comfortable, she might as well get it over with now. She didn't want to live as some awkward conversational obstacle. She didn't want others to pity her and hold their tongues for the short duration she had left in this life, finally able to breathe a guilty sigh of relief when she passed on.

*Oh well, at least we can talk about things again.*

Fuck that. She wasn't having any of it.

"You used to be spiritual, Ritz," she said. "I know it wasn't like what 49 believes, but what do you think?"

She watched him squirm in his seat and suspected that it wasn't just the mechanically supported lung in his chest causing him discomfort.

"I don't know..." he said noncommittally. "I guess there could be *something* after death. Who am I to say?"

"You're Riyaad Tariq," Raquel said. "Captain of the Leopold. Former inhabitant of Morgiana, raised in the Alnabatist order. You have just as much right to say as anyone."

Ritz made a face, inhaling slowly. He looked down at the mini console that was built into the arm of his seat, scrolled through something, then looked up at the ceiling.

"I don't know," he repeated. "If you're asking what I think, what I *really think*, then no. I don't think there's anything after this. I think the energy that animates your life is dispersed back into the universe when you die. And if you're lucky, it can feed the next living thing after you. Maybe you feed the soil on some distant planet or scavengers make a meal out of you. I know it sounds morbid but to me, it's about being useful after death. That's what I believe in. That's what I want."

"If I may ask," 49 said. "Why did you relinquish your faith?"

Ritz took another deep breath and leaned back.

"Ya know, I wish I could say that something truly great or terrible happened to open my eyes to the nature of the universe. I wish I could say I was enlightened and ascended beyond that sort of superstitious thinking. But the truth is, I used to believe that everything could—*somewhere* down the line—be fixed. I believed that no matter how bad things got you could always find your way back. Then one day," he shrugged. "I just found that I didn't believe that anymore."

The room was quiet for a moment as everyone thought about that. Nadia began tapping lightly on the floor again with her knife.

"What about you, Nadia?" Ritz asked, passing the question. "Do you believe in an afterlife?"

There was a final *tick* as Nadia stopped tapping.

"I don't know what the next mission is," she said precisely. "I don't know if there *is* a next mission. But if there is, I'll be ready to take my orders." Nadia pointed the knife at Byzzie. "If I gotta answer then so do you, girl."

Byzzie sighed, still facing away from the group. Then she spun to face them.

"Wanna know what I believe? I believe there's a Hell. I think everybody has one inside of them, and given the right circumstances, they're just dying to invite others in."

11
_______

## FIRST STEPS INTO HELL

Charlene Banks raked the sights of her Neural Rifle over the room in front of her. Indigo Squad was standing in the middle of what appeared to be an employee break room. A fridge sat humming off to one side. A few circle tables were laying at odd angles with their respective chairs sticking legs-up like an animal in rigor mortis. Considering all of the commotion that had taken place here, she could only find one bloodstain.

Off in the back corner by the door that led into the next hallway, there was a dark brown patch. The door itself had been clawed off of its hinges along with the one they had just come through. Charlene could see the scene take place in her mind.

One person hiding in the corner. The hostiles break through the door. The survivor tries to run for it but is cut down before reaching their escape.

The scene had been all too common since they had entered the building. Not only had numerous hostiles entered the hospital through any entryway they could find or create but judging by the state of some of the rooms and how the doors were laying, some had come from inside as well.

It made sense when she thought about it. There could be any number of dead or dying people in a hospital, so when the pulse wave hit this was likely one of the first establishments to go down.

*Figures that fucking Jackson would have to bury her Light Core beneath it.*

Charlene worked through it as the team continued down out into the hallway. She had fought numerous militant factions that would place high-value targets beneath hospitals or schools. At first, she had thought it was an ill-fated attempt at using civilians as human shields.

The PUC didn't care though. When it came to their orders, the greater good always outweighed individual lives. That was the only way to operate. In her time, she had executed families; tortured children in front of their parents to extract information; and even gone so far as to destroy whole towns or villages after a mission as a warning to others: *If you shelter terrorists in any way, then you are a terrorist.*

So as she operated, it slowly became clear that militias didn't place high-value targets around places sure to yield high civilian casualties to dissuade attack but rather to maximize the targets' value if they were to be destroyed. And that value would be maximized through recruitment materials.

All it took was for someone taking illegal pictures nearby to blow the images up into posters, plaster some bold red letters on the side, and use them as damning evidence against the PUC. The message would be clear.

*The PUC kills children. The PUC bombs hospitals. You're not safe. No one is.*

The reality of the matter was that the messages were true. The PUC did do all those things, but for a higher purpose that was obscured by the crude propaganda.

And as far as Charlene knew, no one had found a good way around that. They still had to hit those high-value targets. They still had to send a message of fear and power to the civilian population through demonstrations of extreme force. The problem was, there would always be a small percentage that would latch onto those actions and become prime for radicalization by any militant groups willing to put in the work of recruitment. It was the eternal struggle and Charlene didn't see it being resolved within her lifetime.

As Indigo Squad worked their way through the empty rooms and hallways, Charlene was glad that for just this once, the SEUs weren't the bad guys. Not that what she thought she did on a regular basis was wrong—she wholeheartedly believed in the mission—but for once it was a relief to being doing something that likely wouldn't draw criticism from the general public.

Charlene knew she shouldn't let it get to her but it did. Any sort of criticism of PUC operations was illegal as it constituted a threat to the common welfare of the people the PUC protected, but in the whispered corners of bars and sitting rooms, she knew what kinds of words were exchanged.

Baby killers. Boogeymen. The SEU program was technically a secret but everyone knew it existed and everyone knew its purpose. They equalized. Anyone or anything that might tip the delicate balance of the state was a threat to everyone under the state, and therefore needed to be dealt with by any means necessary. The job was brutal, merciless, and—in the eyes of critics—a gross violation of individual rights.

Charlene knew the theoretical justification—knew that collective rights outweighed the rights of individuals in the way that the death of a single person was of less consequence than the deaths of ten. The math was simple. But that wasn't what drove her.

What drove her was her unit. Her family. The only people she had shared her life with since birth. She would protect them and die for them regardless of any ideology or external motivation. The only people that could hold any sort of candle to that relationship were their handlers. Handlers' roles were closer to that of parents than commanding officers. While being both authoritarian and disciplinarian, they were also gentle and empathetic; inspiring what essentially amounted to familial bonds.

And Charlene had lost family today. Joaner. The wisecracking, lighthearted one of the squad. He was gone now. Dead. Killed by a traitor, a separatist, and an enemy of the state. If anyone ever deserved killing, it was those two. Kit and Nadia. Nadia was beyond their reach and Kit...well, Kit's time was coming. One way or another.

But that was for later. Right now, they were mission-focused.

The hospital seemed to groan around them like an empty belly as they descended lower and lower into the building. She felt cool. Comfortable. This was her wheelhouse. Her team was at her back. Though down by two at the moment, three SEUs were still a nigh-unstoppable force in these tight quarters. Granted, the enemy they were facing was formidable but they were also big and tended to clump together. She wasn't about to make the rookie mistake of firing at groups of them rather than individual targets but the stopping force and rate of fire of the Neural Rifles were so massive as to be almost unnecessary. Unlike the energy bolts fired by the standard-issue PUC energy rifles, one round from a Neural Rifle at full power was enough to punch through 9 inches of concrete. And as hard as these things' outer shells seemed to be, they weren't anywhere near being able to withstand that sort of firepower.

"Looks pretty dead in there," James said over the comms.

"Looks that way," Charlene replied. They had just hit the second sub-level of the hospital and were descending further via the stairs.

"This place was crawling when we passed by earlier. Where did they all go?"

The question hung in the air as Indigo pressed on. Then, the stairway ended.

"Hey, Vanessa, didn't you say there were four levels?" Charlene had been counting as they went down. Just to confirm, she looked at the painted white number on the last doorway, illuminating a giant "B3."

"There is." A beat of silence. "Are you sure you went down the Northeast stairwell?"

"Affirmative," Charlene said. "And are you telling me that only one staircase goes all the way down?"

No answer from the other side. Charlene could feel the woman thinking on the other end. Knew that the question hadn't really been a question, but rather an attempt to reconcile the situation with what she was certain of.

"Charlene." Vanessa's voice was low. Cautious. "Can you tilt the cam back down at the floor?"

Charlene felt a chill run up her back. Slowly, she tilted her helmet down.

The floor was almost even. Almost. At the edges, there was the slight curvature of a ridge, as if they were seeing the top of a very large rubber balloon. There was also something strange about the color. Her helmet couldn't do much for coloring in the low light but the floor also looked darker here than in other places.

"Something made this," Charlene said. The SEUs immediately backed up onto the stairs. Then, kneeling. Charlene reach down and knocked on the hard dark material. "It looks like they blocked off our path downward."

"Can you cut through it?" Vanessa asked.

"Let me see..." The whir of small machinery came from the left gauntlet on Charlene's Arc Suit and a small plasma torch emerged from the area just below her wrist. There was a snap and a sharp, blue flame sprang to life.

The dark material was dense and glossy like a thick plastic. Charlene slowly dragged the flame in a tight line down the resin's surface and it bubbled away. Two minutes later, there was a dull thud as a five-by-five foot square of the hard material dropped to the ground below, revealing a hole through which they could jump.

Charlene looked down into the black, and as she stared, the curved outlines of organic structures slowly took shape as her helmet illuminated the area.

"What do you think is down there?" James muttered from off to her right.

"I'm not sure," Charlene responded. "I think we're going to check it out though."

"Be careful," James said over the comms. "If things go sideways, you get the hell out of there."

"I'll remind everyone that we *need* to activate that Light Core," Vanessa added. "If we don't do it soon, we'll be answering to however many ships are left hanging over us."

Charlene could feel the tension in the comms center even from so many miles away. It was a tension that permeated the whole of what the SEUs were. The tension between the mission and the unit—that is, the cohesive unit that made up their squad. She had learned, however, that the two couldn't be regarded as being at odds with each other. For in the end, the unit was the mission and the mission was the unit. The tension between the two simply acted as a binding agent.

But now there was something that didn't belong and something that was missing. Joaner, her brother, was missing. And Vanessa Jackson, this traitor, didn't belong. Sure, their objectives temporarily aligned but the second that they no longer did, the woman would be eliminated. There simply wasn't room for her or her state of mind. Not in the unit. Not in the PUC. Not anywhere in the whole universe.

"Going down," Charlene said, the words slicing through any hesitancy that lingered in her.

One by one, Indigo Squad plunged into darkness.

**12**

---

## THE GAIA SPINE

Ritz felt his jaw stiffen tighter and tighter the nearer they got to the Gaia Spine.

At first, the long line of what had once been the Earth appeared as nothing more than a minuscule line. One could have even mistaken it for a hair or crack on the surface of the viewport. But then, as it began to take shape, the magnificence of the dance of colors around them slowly seemed to fade to the background.

Suspended in open space, as if on some long invisible wire, was an endless line of shattered and pulverized rocks, dirt, trees, and vegetation. The scale of it was deceivingly large. What looked like mere human-sized portions of ground covered in green grew and grew until whole forests, rivers, and deserts could be made out on top.

And right at the center of the viewport hung what appeared to be a massive mountain range. At its summit was a large deciduous forest, its trees massive—almost as massive as the trees on his home planet of Morgiana. And as the Leopold drew up to skim along the top, Ritz observed the occasional flight of huge birds, the likes of which he had never seen.

"I never knew..." Byzzie breathed out.

"No one does," 49 said. "The only reason I do is that I'm one of the few sentient beings that has emerged from the Void after being fully submerged. My time spent there—if you could call it that—exposed me to a vast number of secrets regarding this new wilderness of ours. The problem is, I can't exactly rattle them all off in quick succession. Each insight or map exists as a memory. Each memory is like a room to a new house I have yet to enter."

"So where are we headed?" Ritz asked.

"To the end of the line," He pointed at the top of the mountain. As they approached, the light inside of the ship began to increase. Shadows shrank and colors that had once been dull now emitted a sort of vital energy. And not only that but the worn and haggard appearance of everyone onboard began to relax into a youthful ease.

"What's happening?" Raquel asked. Ritz understood immediately. It wasn't just the appearance of things. It was the *feel*. Weariness and anxiety seemed to slide off of him like old clothes. The stale air of the cockpit suddenly tasted like the water from a crisp mountain stream after a grueling hike through the desert.

Ritz turned and looked at 49 and what he saw only served to elevate his confusion. The android was glowing. Not just the silver that covered the majority of his body but the gold of his eyes and mouth shone with a brilliance the likes of which he had scarcely dreamt of. He seemed at once the android they had known while also appearing to be completely reborn, as if hundreds of years had passed and aged him like wine.

49 turned towards them, a look of pure serenity on his face. "I do not know," he replied.

There was a sudden jolt, snapping them out of their reverie. And then Ritz realized something else. There was something there, buried beneath all of the reverie and wonder. Something so fleeting that he thought he had imagined it.

A sorrow. A weight.

"What was that?" Byzzie said, looking around dazed. She tapped at her screen. "What happened?"

"I think we landed," 49 said hesitantly. There was a dense fog in front of the viewport, but as it began to clear, an open field was revealed before them. Fragile ankle-high grass swayed as a gentle breeze glided down between jutting stone cliffs on either side. A few trees stood in the field, their flowers a translucent pink. And there in the middle of the field stood a stone archway, each of its asymmetrical halves were bisected by a foot wide gap. There were no markings or anything to indicate that it had been placed there by people, but there was also something about it. Not unnatural per se, but hyper-natural. Seeing it for the first time, Ritz felt as if he was experiencing a long-lost memory from his childhood and by the looks of it, the rest of the crew were having the same reaction.

Moving as if walking on air, the crew exited the Leopold. Ritz felt light-headed as he walked down the ship's narrow hallway and wasn't sure how to feel about that. On one hand, he could have been having the same reaction that everyone else seemed to be having. On the other, it was possible that his lungs were finally beginning to malfunction and his brain wasn't getting enough oxygen. He made a note to talk to the nurse about that later.

What was her name again? Amelia. That sounded right.

Almost as if on cue, Ritz saw the old woman's head peer tentatively out of King's living quarters. He had seen her briefly when she had boarded the ship back on Desia and Raquel had been right, she was old. But seeing her now—her silver hair tied back in a neat bun, posture erect, clear and direct eye contact as she met his gaze—he noticed a strong vitality in her.

After stepping out into the hallway, she was followed by a short stocky woman with a thick midsection that looked like she could pull the Leopold across the tarmac of a landing pad with her teeth. Then right behind her was a dark-eyed man that moved with the fluidity of some wild carnivorous mammal. Both were wearing matching olive green armor and carrying compact ZT140 energy rifles with holographic sights.

"Captain Tariq," Amelia said. "We left Desia in such a hurry that we didn't get to introduce ourselves. My name is Amelia. This here is Samantha and Marcus."

"Welcome aboard," Ritz said. "Unfortunately we don't have time to chat. We need to secure a perimeter around the ship as soon as possible."

"You heard the man," Amelia said, nodding at the two soldiers. "Hop to it."

Without another word, Samantha and Marcus turned and walked purposefully down the hall toward the ship's exit ramp.

*Chatty pair*, Ritz thought to himself. He knew he had just said they didn't have time to talk but if he hadn't have known better, it seemed as if the pair were taking orders from Amelia, not him.

Moving up to the open door the three had just exited, Ritz popped his head around the corner and said, "King, you coming with?"

"Unfortunately, King will not be joining you on this mission," Amelia explained. "As we were leaving the Pillon System, King's heart rate became erratic. I don't expect there's much to worry about—most likely a combination of pain and fatigue—but I gave him a mild sedative, and he's getting some much-needed rest."

"Bullshit. We need King out there," Ritz said, but even as he made his way further into the mechanic's living quarters, he could see that the man was indeed resting peacefully in his bunk, his right leg bandaged and elevated.

"Fine," he relented. "But you're staying on board with him. Are you armed?"

"I am a healer, Captain Tariq. I have no need to arm myself."

*Great,* Ritz thought to himself. *Another one.*

The euphoria he had felt upon landing had almost completely vanished and been replaced by a dull throb at the center of his forehead. When Vanessa had offered to lend them a nurse, he had expected a soft, kind old lady; not this bulldog of a woman.

Ritz put a fist to his forehead and mashed his eyes shut for a second, then he opened them again. "Look: I'm thankful you're here. I know coming along with us probably wasn't your first choice. But on my ship, I—stop. What's this? What are you doing?"

While Ritz had been talking, Amelia began fiddling with the dials on Ritz's silver lung contraption. Suddenly, there was a light hiss and Ritz felt something like a knot of tension release in his chest, which then spread up his neck and into his head.

"Your MBA needed readjusting," the woman explained. "Now, you can go out there but you *must* be careful. This isn't some chest plate or piece of armor you're wearing. This is a temperamental piece of equipment. So no running, jumping, or slamming into things. And *definitely* don't let this take a bullet or energy bolt. Or you will *die* Mr. Tariq."

With equal parts relief and frustration warring in his head, Ritz exhaled slowly, letting the oxygen flow freely through his system for what felt like the first time in hours.

"I'm letting a lot slide right now simply because I don't have time for it," he finally said as calmly as he could. "But when we're done down there, we're going to be having a conversation. Understood?"

"Understood," Amelia replied, and to Ritz's astonishment, there was no trace of combativeness in her tone. "Until then, I'll stay here and make sure your friend is taken care of. You can count on me."

"Thank you, Amelia." And with that, the captain of the Leopold joined the rest of his crew outside.

Upon exiting, Ritz observed that 49 had, in fact, very softly *crashed* their ship. The vessel didn't look any worse for wear, especially considering the beating it had taken from the giant bugs back on Desia, but the whole thing lay somewhat lopsided on its belly, the landing gear undeployed.

Ritz shook his head as a wave of nausea washed over him. Despite whatever Amelia had done onboard, he was still far from being at his best. Feeling something in his chest spasm, Ritz stopped and grimaced as forks of red-hot pain coursed through him. When the feeling finally subsided, he took a look around at the area where they had landed.

The crew of the Leopold were spread out in a loose circle, creating a perimeter around the ship. 49 and Nadia were near the front of the group, being flanked by Raquel on the right and Byzzie on the left. Then off to the rear, Samantha was kneeling on the ground, scanning the area over the sights of her energy rifle. Marcus, on the other hand, was nowhere to be seen. That wasn't surprising, Ritz figured, as he was probably on the other side of the ship, and after conferring with Nadia over the comms, he confirmed as much.

"What do we do?" Raquel asked as he strode up to the front. More than anyone else, she looked energized. As if some great weight had been removed.

"I suppose," 49 said, lifting a finger. "We walk through that." He pointed at the arch.

An outside observer might have been forgiven for thinking that the stone arch was simply what it looked like: two pieces of rock lying in the middle of the field. Nothing in front of it and nothing beyond. But there was an electricity to the place, a current that seemed to flow toward it. In fact, Ritz thought to himself, the feeling wasn't all that unlike the feeling of the pulse wave that had hit Desia and brought the dead back to life.

It was different though. It felt cleaner. Less corrupted.

"You sure about this, 49?" Ritz asked.

"I'm not sure about anything," replied the android, predictably.

*Nothing ventured.*

Ritz started forward. His body labored, his lungs aching occasionally. And while the pain and fatigue he felt now was certainly less than what it may have felt like in some other... less *enchanted* place, it was still present. But still, he forged on, the others falling in behind him.

As they got closer, Ritz caught a glimpse of movement

out of the corner of his eye. He froze, everyone freezing with him. Nothing moved. No one spoke.

A gentle breeze picked up, rustling the leaves of the trees around them, and then subsided again.

"What is it?" 49 said, his voice a whisper. The android was nearly ten feet away, but the place was so quiet that his voice carried the distance.

"I don't think we're alone," Ritz replied, his hand dropping down to his holster.

The leaves rustled again, but this time there was no wind. The sound seemed to come from every direction and then it was gone.

Ritz stepped gingerly forward, his eyes picking apart the scenery around them. Aside from the small trees, there was nowhere to hide, and even those offered little cover. He felt his foot on the soft earth, the crisp air in his lungs. The weapon at his side seemed to vibrate with its own intention.

Slowly, the rest of his crew turned their gaze outward as they too continued forward.

"What is this place?" Ritz asked, mostly to himself. "What are we doing here?"

The answer was obvious. 49 had explained both their reason for coming and the origins of the place itself. That, however, did nothing to increase their understanding of the environment they had just stepped into. There were still so many questions like: why did this place give off the feeling of being drugged? What exactly kept the broken pieces of the once whole planet in line? And most importantly: what lived here now that the world had ended? What creature could call this place its home?

They were a mere 25 feet from the arch now. The wind had died almost completely. No sounds or flashes of movement. 49 had moved up and positioned himself closest to the structure as the circle of them gradually grew together and rotated, each individual member searching for whoever or whatever dwelled at the border of their sight and hearing.

"I'm not sure we should-" 49 began, but before he could finish there was a chorus of loud nearly simultaneous snaps as the world seemed to fly into motion.

Tiny pink flowers disappeared almost instantly as they folded in on themselves. Dry limbs stretched and sprang to life as rooted feet dislodged themselves from the earth. Moving faster than anything Ritz had ever seen, they were on them.

The tree was almost ten feet away, but in a blink of an eye, branches as strong as steel whipped across his skin and fastened him into place. He tried to lift his legs but they were held so tightly that he might as well have been fighting the very essence of gravity itself. He felt his fingers hovering there, touching his sidearm but unable to draw it. He frantically looked around and found every one of his crew in more or less the same position. Some had their guns drawn and some didn't, but the effect was the same. They were caught. The very trees around them locking them to the Earth like so many stones.

———

"WHERE ARE THEY?" James asked, tension thick in his voice. Charlene felt it too. The anticipation for a battle that should have come and ended ten times over by now.

"They're down here," Charlene said. All of the instruments built into her suit were quiet. No motion. No far-off noises of things scrabbling around. Nothing. But there was something in the air. In the floor. The walls. A sort of spatial vibration one feels when they enter a dark room and can instantly tell that someone's in there with them. They were here.

As far as she could tell, they had been moving steadily down for some time now. They should have hit the final floor of the hospital by now but they hadn't. The tunnels just kept going.

Wherever they were headed, it wasn't in the hospital.

"How are we looking up there?" Charlene asked.

"Still doing okay," Hutchens answered, his voice crackling in her ear. "None of the vessels have taken up any sort of offensive position, but they're still moving around, so not all of 'em are dead in the water. I don't know how much time we have, so don't dawdle."

"Well, we may have a bit of a problem," Charlene said. "I don't think we're in the hospital anymore. It feels like we're underground. Like, properly underground. The bugs must have burrowed in."

"What?" Came Hutchens' voice, thick with alarm. "Are you sure?"

"Not entirely. I've never been in this hospital before. But it doesn't feel like it. It feels too deep below the surface."

"Well, can you double back?" Hutchens asked.

"We can," Charlene replied, "But I didn't see any branching passageways that might lead back in the direction we'd need to go. They all seem to be angled down."

"Okay." There was a beat of silence as Hutchens thought things over on the other end. Then, "Go back to the third sub-level and see if you can access it. From there, you'll just have to cut through the floor."

"Wait," came Jackson's voice over the comms. "The level you need still has to be close. Go find one of the branching passageways and take it. You should eventually end up where you need to."

Charlene had to hand it to the woman, for being a disorganized separatist, she could deliver an order with just as much conviction and weight as the colonel. Unfortunately for her though, there wasn't a choice. Charlene didn't even hesitate.

"Heading back to sub-level 3," Charlene confirmed, overriding Jackson. Given the choice between the colonel and Head of Desian Defense, Charlene would pick the colonel every time.

"Stop," Jackson commanded, but before she got any further, there was a blur of motion and Charlene was knocked off of her feet. Green Neural Rifle fire exploded around her and in the strobing light, all Charlene could see was a wall of undulating serrated legs.

Catapulting back to her feet, she aimed at the nearest one and pulled the trigger.

———

RITZ STRUGGLED against his bonds with little effect. The branches squeezed tighter and tighter until he finally had to cease moving, for fear that they would crush his breathing device. Off to his left, he heard a groan and a snap and when he looked, he saw Nadia slowly forcing her right arm upward, the branch that had wrapped itself around her beginning to break.

In an instant, she slammed her hand back down, just as she ignited the blue plasma blade on her right gauntlet, and there was a low guttural groan as she sliced through the branches and deep into the trunk of the tree. Fire and smoke hissed as she twisted the blade and plunged it deeper.

"Cease." The voice was less of a cry and more of a thunderclap. Distinctly male, it had a grit and volume to it that seemed almost superhuman. Everyone froze in place except for Nadia, who continued to sink the plasma blade deeper into the tree.

Ritz twisted his head to see if he could see who had spoken but couldn't quite get the angle right. Whoever was speaking was behind him. What was more, they seemed to also be somewhere above them, up in the air. Ritz felt a tingling at the base of his neck as the air surged with static electricity.

"*Cease!*" The voice repeated, and almost immediately after there was a blinding flash and Nadia rocketed backward, flipping end over end. There was a loud *thump* as her body hit the ground and lay there motionless, smoke rising off of her.

"Nadia!" Ritz cried, struggling once again. But before the tree could fasten itself any tighter, he caught sight of who had spoken and froze in place.

The voice had sounded as if it had come from a man but the thing that landed looked about as far from a man as Ritz could possibly imagine.

The thing alighted in a heavy flurry of wings, two of which swept the air at its back and two of which seemed to be placed over its body. The harder Ritz stared, the harder it was to look at. Still, he got an impression of faces. To his surprise, there was the face of a man. In addition to this, there was also the face of a large predatory cat, some huge bird of prey, and a horned bull. And all around the creature spun multiple burning wheels.

Smoke arose from the area where the thing had landed,

and as it turned its gaze on Ritz, the captain involuntarily forced his face down as if someone had just turned on a blinding light in a dark room. As he glanced down, however, he noticed that the creature's legs were straight and ended with something like a hoof.

The thing stretched its arms and wings, and as it did, it seemed to shine like polished bronze. As he cowered, Ritz felt like the world around him was bending inward, enfolding him. More than the tree, but the earth itself. He also noticed that at some point the wind had picked up and was all but pulverizing the lot of them.

Then, just as quickly as the whole scene had begun, it ended.

The wind died. The branches of the tree loosened. Life seemed to flow back into the world where nothing but fear had occupied it moments before. Blinking rapidly, Ritz carefully lifted his gaze to the creature as it stood in the center of them.

Its wings appeared to be folding back as its other inhuman features softened and sank into its body. Ritz felt the muscles in his forehead and face relax as the intensity of the thing lessened. Even so, he got the impression that this wasn't real—that the transformation that had taken place before his eyes was actually an illusion, like hallucinating at the edge of sleep.

Ritz finally felt the tree branches around him slacken and he fell to the ground, feeling as if all the energy had just been swiftly knocked out of him. Looking around, he saw that everyone looked to be having roughly the same experience. Raquel was on her hands and knees holding her neck. Samantha and Byzzie were both bent over as they tried to catch their breath. Even Marcus could be seen as he stumbled around the nose of the ship hefting his weapon and trying to focus. The only one that looked remotely okay was 49, who seemed to be staring at the figure with a sort of shocked wonderment. The only one that wasn't up and moving was Nadia.

Fighting his way up and onto his feet, Ritz clumsily drew his sidearm.

"Nadia," he tried to shout the word but it came out as a sort of desperate cough. He tried to focus but as he stumbled forward, he lost his balance and fell back onto the soft earth. At some point, he must have let go of his weapon, because when he made it back onto his feet again his hands were empty.

The figure that had descended upon them was now striding over to where Nadia lay in the grass. Its current form moved gracefully with an underlying sense of power.

"You stay away from her," Ritz choked. He stopped and turned around, searching for his fallen pistol, but as he did the world seemed to tilt sideways and he suddenly found himself doubled over and vomiting.

When he had finished, he felt his head begin to clear. Out of the corner of his eye, he saw Byzzie trying to raise the small submachine gun she had brought with her from the ship, but every time she tried to raise it her arms seemed to go limp and drop back down to her sides.

Determined to do it himself, Ritz tried once again to reclaim his sidearm and this time he found it lying in the grass just an inch shy of the pool of vomit. He quickly snatched the pistol up and, trying not to overthink it or let himself fall victim to whatever haze had descended upon him and his crew, he tried forcing the sights of the pistol on the figure. As he did however, he understood why Byzzie was having such a hard time.

Right as the sights began to line up, his eyes felt as if

they were being flooded with light. His face slackened and his wrists lost all of their strength. Then the next thing he knew, his hands were back down at his sides.

"You will not succeed in hurting me," the creature said. It had reached Nadia and was now kneeling down beside her. It placed a hand on her back and Ritz saw the gentle rise and fall of steady breaths. "If I wanted to kill her, I would have. She is merely resting now."

Then, before Ritz could think of something to say, 49 beat him to the punch.

"What are you?" He asked. And as he did, Ritz was struck by how simultaneously human yet artificial the android's voice sounded. There was certainly an element of awe in his tone, but underneath it was a sort of metallic pang that Ritz had failed to notice until now.

"I am the Way Keeper," the creature replied. "Guardian of the *Brokk di Fen*. However, you may call me Nakir. This is the name by which these earthly creatures address me." Nakir stretched out his arm, gesturing at the trees.

"These trees tried to kill us," Byzzie declared. She seemed to have given up trying to aim at the creature but was still gripping her weapon tight.

"They merely detained you," Nakir declared. "We have not had visitors here for an age. They are welcoming but not without caution."

"What..." 49 began. He was standing up straight now but seemed to be involuntarily leaning toward the new arrival, like a moth drawn to a flame. "..are you," he finally managed to say. Then, "I mean...are you a man or..."

"Are you a man?" Nakir asked, suddenly turning around. Something like anger seemed to slip in the figure's face and Ritz froze where he was standing. "Wide thorax. Narrow pelvis. Short torso. It appears as if you have been formed roughly in the male image, but tell me? Do you reproduce? Did you choose these traits or were they a part of you all along? Tell me, 49, what are *you*? What have you become? What were you created to be?"

49 seemed shocked to silence, and if Ritz could have chosen any of them to have had an answer to these questions, he would have picked the android that was now standing dumbstruck before him.

"I suppose," 49 began hesitantly. "My programming was based on the historical phenomenological traits of men. Therefore, it is not inaccurate to say I am a man."

Nakir strode over to where 49 was standing and placed a hand on his chest.

"You speak with uncertainty," he said, then he removed his hand. "I, however, will not: you are not a man." It looked like he was done but then Nakir said, "the use of a double-negative from an android though is...curious."

"Curious?" 49 tilted his head. "In what way?"

"I cannot see you, android. I cannot see your heart yet you appear to have one. It is veiled before me. If you had not been here then I would not have arrived in such a dramatic fashion. Your presence however is troubling. There is not a lot in this world that I do not see, yet this has been withheld. Why? And by whom?"

At this, 49 looked genuinely shocked. It looked like he had further questions but Ritz cut him off.

"Nakir, we've come to shut down the Light Wire Network. Can you help us?"

Best to keep it simple, Ritz thought.

"I see your purpose, Riyaad Tariq, and it has been judged righteous. The path, however, is not an easy one. So you must decide for yourself and those around you: will you walk it?"

"Allow me," 49 interjected. "I can take whatever it is you have laid out before us. If it is a sacrifice you ask, then-"

"Hold your tongue," snapped Nakir. "This path must be endured by a human soul. What you seek cannot be attained by the likes of you."

The words seemed to hit 49 like a hail of bullets. Ritz watched him rock where he stood, as if what Nakir had said had a literal physical weight.

"I will do it," Ritz said.

"You do not know what it entails."

"I will do it," he repeated. "Everything hangs in the balance. If we fail here then we'll drown in those monsters. We *have* to succeed."

"Wait," Raquel said. "Why can't I do it? Or Samantha or Marcus? Ritz is injured, worse than most of us."

Nakir turned toward Ritz. "Are you their leader?"

Ritz hesitated. "They are their own masters. I do not make choices for them."

"But they have chosen to follow you."

"Yes," Ritz finally said. "They have."

"Then you are their leader." Nakir walked over to where he was standing. Ritz tried to look up at him but found it difficult. He reached out and placed a hand on Ritz's chest, just to the right of his breathing apparatus.

"I see you," he said, dropping his voice. "I see your past. I see the things you have done. The way forward is hard. You may not come back. If you do, then you won't be the same."

"Okay," Ritz said, steadying himself. "Where am I going? What would you like me to do."

"Follow me." Nakir lifted a hand and pointed at the stone archway. "Into death."

## 13

## THE BROKEN PASSAGE

Indigo was lost in the dark.

Below ground in a tunnel dug by monsters, they were now fighting for their lives. They didn't know the way forward. Their path back was blocked. All around them was clattering, chittering razor-sharp death.

And Charlene was not concerned.

Black blood and chitinous armor were blasted apart in front of her as she held down the trigger on her Neural Rifle, released it, and then held it down again. The stock of the weapon pounded her shoulder armor as she poured round after round into the oncoming horde. She brought down one, two, three, four of them. Aware of her ammunition, she swung the barrel and gunned down two more.

Pollie and Weaver had begun firing before her and were close to running dry. Though the three of them operated as a single unit, the two of them were alternating fire in a way that would result in Pollie running out of ammunition first. In the time it would take her to reload, Weaver would be able to cover her until he ran dry as well. Once his gun was empty, they would swap roles and she would then cover him.

Charlene recognized it as the three-part Primrose Form —an attack pattern they had practiced a million times over the years. It featured an evolving pattern of covering and reloading between three SEUs in a close-combat situation. The form evolved differently depending on the strength, numbers, and lethal reach of their targets but Charlene instinctively assessed the situation and reacted accordingly.

After emptying her rifle, she swung it around and locked it onto the mag-clamps on her back. As she brought her arm back around she unclipped her melee weapon from her hip. Readying herself, she heard Pollie's rifle run out. Pollie then began backing up as she reloaded. Weaver took point, blasting two incoming Necrosarks, his Neural Rifle clicking dry at the end. The second one didn't go down, however, and as the wounded creature readied itself for another attack, Weaver stepped in and booted it directly in the face.

He could have gone in with a follow-up to finish the monster off but this would have left him open to an attack from one of the other countless monsters in the area. Instead, he backed off as Pollie finished reloading, who then brought her gun up and put two rounds through the Necrosark's head.

Seeing her opportunity, Charlene rocketed forward and leaped between the two other SEUs. More attackers were pushing in and when she landed, Charlene tagged three Necrosarks within the kill zone. The closest one was to her left, the second to her right, and the third one was charging right up the middle. She waited a crucial half-second and then flew into motion.

Her melee weapon was a dual-bladed plasma staff with a folding handle. As soon as the right moment arrived,

Charlene snapped the handle up and the two halves unfolded and locked into a single piece. She then depressed the toggle switch as she swung upward and a single white blade shot out of the end just as it came within range of the nearest Necrosark and sliced vertically up through its head. Not wasting a single moment, she spun around and brought the super-heated blade down on the second attacker, killing it as well. The third one was already there though, rearing up and preparing its own attack.

Charlene pivoted, took one step back, and brought the staff up to fend off the blows. The blade caught the monster in the middle of its foreleg with enough force to knock it aside, leaving a thread of burned sinew dangling behind. Stepping in for the counter, Charlene hit another toggle and the second blade snapped to life at the opposite end of the staff. Already sensing more attackers pressing in, she stabbed the blade up into the monster's neck, twisted, and swiftly drew it back out, decapitating it in a spray of black blood.

Green jets of Neural Rifle fire lanced through the air on both her left and right and were accompanied by the screams of more dying Necrosarks. She spun the blade around and prepared for more.

The whole time they had been fighting, the three SEUs had slowly but steadily been moving deeper and deeper underground. The attack had come from behind them, meaning that the Necrosarks had circled around and were likely herding them forward. Into what, Charlene had no idea, but as Indigo slowly shook off the shock of the initial wave and fought to regain the advantage, they also slowed their descent into the passageways until they were finally fighting at a stand-still. As soon as they were, Charlene's comms burped and she heard James's voice.

"Indigo press forward. Make your way to sub-level 3."

"Affirmative," Charlene replied as she swung the plasma blade around her head in a wide sweeping arc, killing two Necrosarks in a single blow. A third one reared up out of the blackness, its horrid features illuminated in the white light of her plasma blades. Before she could do anything, its face disappeared in a spray of black blood and green rifle fire.

Without another word, Indigo began to push their way back up to the surface, carving through the endless horde in front of them. That was when another wave hit them from behind.

———

Vanessa watched from the comm center as Indigo Squad attempted to fight a battle from both the front and the back. It was difficult to tell what was going on through the helmet cams but even so, she caught flashes of Necrosarks being stabbed, gutted, and blown apart. She knew the Marauders were competent warriors but this was a real test.

As far as she was concerned, they needed to be good but not *too* good.

"They're moving quickly now," Hutchens said. "They'll be back at the tunnel entrance soon and then we should be back on track."

"They've already looped behind them once," Vanessa interjected. "What if they do it again?"

"What do you mean?"

"I mean, what if the Necrosarks circle around and cut them off? Indigo could fight their way past one of those branching passageways and get flanked. Then they'd be fighting a battle on three sides. They're good, but without you there, James, I don't think they can handle that."

Hutchens seemed to think about that for a moment. Vanessa looked over at Goff who seemed to be deep in thought. She did, however, notice that the top of his holster had silently come unsnapped in the last few minutes.

"What do you propose?" James asked cautiously, his voice level.

Vanessa swallowed and composed herself. "I propose they reverse directions. Continue down. Keep them on their toes. The Necrosarks seem to be adapting to their movements, so if we keep switching it up it will keep them from being able to fully organize."

"Organize," James repeated. "Vanessa, what are you doing?"

"Excuse me, soldier?"

"I asked you-" the massive Marauder stepped forward, placing a heavy metal hand on Vanessa's shoulder. He leaned down and she saw her blurry reflection in his faceplate. "-what are you doing?"

Silence squeezed the room, the tinny sounds of Neural Rifle fire coming from the monitors as Indigo fought for their lives. Hutchens quietly squared himself to the two of them while Goff eased back in his chair, hand creeping toward the butt of his heavy revolver.

"I don't know what you're referring to," Vanessa declared. "Now get your hand off me before-"

James's powerful hand shoved her so hard she spun out of the comm center chair and fell crashing to the floor. In an instant, she was up and looking down the sights of her sidearm. Hutchens and Goff were up as well, both their guns drawn. Goff was aiming at James while Hutchens seemed to be unsure of where to point his. James on the other hand was looking down the sight of his own pistol, the tiny black barrel staring Vanessa in the eye.

"What the fuck are you doing, soldier?" Hutchens growled.

"Don't pretend like you don't see it," James responded casually.

"See what? All I see is you causing conflict right now where we need to be solid. This could be the most crucial moment of our lives and you're-"

"I'm what," James snapped, his voice full of venom. "I'm apprehending a traitor to the People's Union Coalition? I'm stopping my team from getting killed?"

"You're letting your emotions cloud your judgment," Vanessa said cautiously. "I wasn't the one who killed-"

"Don't even speak his name," James said. "By harboring terrorists in your midst, you are complicit in their actions. That's not what I'm talking about though."

"What *are* you talking about, son?" Hutchens implored. "Let's work this through."

"There's no Light Core beneath the city, is there?" James asked.

Vanessa felt the gun in her hand, her palm slick with sweat. She didn't think she had enough firepower to take down James but she'd try.

"*Is there?*" James yelled.

"Of course there is," Vanessa reassured him.

"Bullshit. You've been trying to force my team deeper and deeper into that nest since you started giving orders. Don't deny it."

"I'm trying to keep your team alive," Vanessa shot back. "And if we don't get back to what we were doing then-"

"Then what? Then my team will extract themselves? Then you'll have an SEU squad to deal with when you try and reclaim power here?"

Vanessa exhaled slowly, trying to steady herself. She

looked over at Hutchens but saw that a seed of doubt had been planted. He wasn't aiming his weapon at her but it had definitely moved further in her direction.

"What is he talking about?" Hutchens asked. Then, "Your orders *have* seemed suspicious."

"That's because there's no Light Core." James said. "It's a trap. Just like this city. Just like this whole planet. It's what she does."

"Vanessa," Hutchens took his finger off the trigger and pointed his weapon at the ceiling. "Look me in the eye and tell me there's a Light Core beneath the hospital. If there isn't, we'll work through it. Despite all the suspicion being thrown around the room right now, we still need you. You're our best chance at maintaining order here on Desia."

"Colonel Hutchens, there *is* a Grade-5 Light Core beneath the city," Vanessa lied.

James was shaking his head. "No, no, no. Bullshit. All bullshit."

A quiet moment passed. Then James keyed the comms.

"Indigo get out of there. Shane? Do it."

Vanessa looked around, confused. "Who's Shane?"

"Shane is the man I have posted outside of Kit's room," James explained. "He's the man who's going to succeed where the first one failed."

And at that, the door to the comm center slid open and two more PUC soldiers walked in, each hefting energy rifles.

---

"You heard the man," Charlene said. She brought her plasma staff down on a Necrosark's stabbing limb just before it reached her, then thrust it forward into the creature's unprotected face. Pulling the blade free, she kicked the monster's thrashing body over and moved in to attack two more that had just skittered around the corner, their mandibles clacking.

The sound of her teammates' rifles blared behind her as Pollie and Weaver retreated. The amount of attackers that Charlene was forced into had lessened somewhat while the waves coming from behind them had increased. At this rate, they still should have been able to make it to sub-level 3 without running out of ammunition, but just barely.

Then from there? They'd have their sidearms and melee weapons, but even if those were to fail, they'd fight their way out of the city with their fists if that was what it took. This mission was over. They were leaving.

It had been far from a sure thing when they had all huddled together before leaving the base. There were two things they knew they had to accomplish: oust Vanessa Jackson as a traitor and regain control of the comm center. Both of those required them to blatantly defy Colonel Hutchens, however, and that was no small thing. They had to have proof. And if not that, then at least reasonable suspicion.

They had that now. The moment Jackson had suggested they continue on into the tunnels, they had known James would pry the truth out of her and he would do it in front of the colonel. And if the colonel resisted? Then he would have to go. It was unfortunate but it wasn't the first time they had killed a PUC official. What mattered was the unit. And the unit was nothing without the mission. And as far as Charlene was concerned, Hutchens had compromised them both.

If they had to get rid of him, it wouldn't be much of a problem. One of the rogue Marauders was off-world while the other one lay unconscious in a hospital bed.

Taking Kit hadn't quite gone as planned. Indigo had worked with a few of the PUC soldiers in Hutchens' platoon back during a covert campaign a few years ago. They were good soldiers with hard, on-the-ground experience who would follow orders and wouldn't flap their mouths while doing it. The problem was that there were only four of them.

So they had set Kit up to take a few bullets to the back and significantly weaken Indigo's opposition. Viewing him as a subpar traitor had been a mistake though, as it slowly became clear that they had underestimated him. Sure, the PUC soldier who had pulled the trigger had the drop on him but Kit was still an SEU with an SEU's instincts and reflexes.

Oh well, one of the other soldiers, Shane something or other, would be finishing the job any minute now. The only problem was that they couldn't get at Nadia.

The tactical solution would have been to let both Kit and Nadia leave Desia onboard the Leopold. That way there'd be little-to-no opposition for them during the inevitable takeover. But they had killed Joaner, their brother. They couldn't let that slide. Not in a million years.

Getting both of them would have been nice but one was a good start. With Kit dead, now Nadia would have to live with the pain of her failure. And for an SEU, the pain of losing a member of your unit was worse than death.

All that was left then was to deal with Kingsbane and the rest of the Desian soldiers. Charlene wasn't very concerned. After all, taking care of terrorists was basically her job. She ate guys like that for breakfast.

Charlene slashed her way through three more Necrosarks. The creatures were big and lanky, taking up a large amount of space in the passageway. This might have been advantageous for the monsters if they were facing normal soldiers as a single attacker could blitz its way through a squad of grunts with ease. The SEUs were a different matter entirely.

The sounds of rifle fire had almost died completely except for the occasional burst as either Pollie or Weaver scored a hit. The intensity of the attack seemed to have lessened significantly. Maybe their numbers were close to being exhausted? It was possible. A lot of people had died in the last 24 hours but a lot of fighting had taken place too. Even if a huge population of those things had materialized from any newly created dead bodies, there was just as good of a chance that they had been killed in the subsequent fighting.

As it turned out, Charlene's hopes were grossly misplaced.

She saw the attack coming about two seconds before it happened. They were just rounding a corner when two tunnels intersected, creating a sort of four-way intersection. It was still pitch black down there and Charlene's helmet was continuing to illuminate the hard lines of the passageway but it was the glow from her plasma staff that gave the creatures away. For advanced as the technology built into her Heads Up Display was, it couldn't articulate shadows. And it was the shadows that alerted her.

The attack came from all four sides and Charlene shouted into her comms just before it hit. The problem was, she realized, the comms were down again. They were being blocked.

With mere moments left to spare, Charlene reached down and primed a remote charge she had secured into the munitions slot on her left thigh. She stopped, her saber out in front of her.

The wave of monsters literally slammed into the three SEUs. Charlene felt a searing pain slice into her left side as one of the monster's lethal legs stabbed past her defenses and skewered her through the abdomen. Gritting her teeth, she pushed her way forward, slicing the attacker's limb off at the joint and then jabbing upward into its eyes. Blood sprayed the three of them as the creature sank back, shrieking. But two more were already there, eager to take its place.

"Take the western passageway," Charlene shouted, hoping she could be heard over the cacophony of battle. After receiving two affirmatives, she began to push her way toward the branching tunnel.

The monsters were thick now, their bodies crammed together. It made them less maneuverable in the narrow tunnels but also harder to cut through. This didn't stop her from trying.

Charlene brought the staff up again and again, slashing at the Necrosarks as they bayed and danced before her, deadly limbs slashing back at her. She couldn't tell if they were getting better at avoiding her attacks or if their combined numbers now made it difficult to get close enough to deliver a killing blow without taking a retaliatory one in turn.

One of them finally got too close and Charlene quickly brought her armored foot down on its leg, causing it to topple forward. She then jumped and impaled it through the middle. Three more Necrosarks were right there, ready to take her head off, but she swiftly withdrew the plasma blade and swung it in a full 360-degree circle, chopping off limbs, mandibles, and pieces of skull.

Seizing the opportunity, Pollie and Weaver forced their way up to her position with a wave of attackers right on their tail. Charlene quickly reached down, drew her sidearm, and emptied the magazine into the oncoming Necrosarks.

The pistol wasn't as fancy as the one Curtis had used to incapacitate Kit but it still did the job. Chambered with a heavy .50 round, the sidearm boomed in Charlene's hand as her armor and Tesla-enhanced body absorbed the recoil. Huge chunks of the monsters tore away in splashes of black blood and as they collapsed, the massive rounds continued on through the creatures behind them.

The attackers coming from the western passage were almost on them at this point and Pollie and Weaver quickly gunned them down before Charlene deactivated her staff, unclipped the primed explosive charge, threw it into the middle of the intersecting passageways, and then swung around the nearest corner with the other two SEUs before detonating it.

Even with their protective Arc Suits on, the heat and pressure were intense. A huge *whump* rocked through the three SEUs as they lay huddled on the ground, followed by a gush of fire. Having forgotten that her armor had been pierced, Charlene cried out as the flames scorched the small area of exposed skin.

Before she had time to acknowledge the wound, however, a deep rumbling shook the earth around them. Charlene tried scrambling to her feet along with the other two SEUs.

They made it five feet down the tunnel before it collapsed in on them.

**14**

***

## BROKK DI FEN

The stone arch jutted out of the ground, infinitely more menacing than it had when the Leopold had arrived. Nakir stood before it, shrouded in some sort of cloak that served to blunt the sheer intensity of his being. He stretched out his hand, oddly human with its five fingers, offering death and judgment.

And possibly salvation.

The fact that the two former things seemed rather certain while the latter did not, was deeply troubling to Ritz.

"Hold on," he said, trying to slow the whole thing down. Trying to give himself space to think. "If I pass through that thing, am I going to die?"

"I said that this path leads to death," the strange creature declared. "You will not surely die, however. No living mortal has ever passed through these gates before. Your fate is uncertain, as it always has been."

Ritz felt out of his depth. He turned to 49 for support.

"This place," the android began. "This...*Brokk di Fen* as

you called it—I think we deserve to know a little more about it before we go blundering in."

"Before Tariq goes blundering in," Nakir corrected.

"Yes, before Ritz enters. What is it? Please tell us more, if you will."

"The *Brokk di Fen* is the path of death and judgment, as I have said. To walk it is to be judged and held accountable for every one of your sins. You will encounter each of them as the victim rather than the perpetrator, and you will bear that weight."

"Okay," Ritz said hesitantly. "I think I can handle that. I'm pretty sure I've done more good than bad in this world. Hopefully, those odds will tip in my favor."

And even as he spoke he realized he fell just short of believing them.

"Unfortunately, that is not how it works. Your good deeds do not counterbalance your bad ones."

"What?" Ritz cried out. "That's not entirely fair then, is it?"

"It is not about fairness," Nakir said. "It is about the debt you incurred by perpetrating harm in a broken world. Tell me, under your own legal systems, if a doctor saves one hundred lives one day yet maliciously takes one the next, is he not tried for murder? Is he not still held accountable for taking that one life despite any good he may have done in the past?"

Ritz chewed on that one a bit, then finally said, "If I do this—if I walk through that—whatever it is, will I be able to shut down the Light Wire Network?"

"After you walk the path, you will come to the Luminary Heart. If you destroy it, then you will destroy the network."

"Good," Ritz declared. "Let's go then." He began walking forward toward the stone arch.

"Wait," 49 said behind him. Ritz turned and saw his crew looking at him, worry writ large on all of their faces.

"Yes?" he asked, trying to keep his own apprehension out of his voice.

For a moment, no one spoke. Then finally, Byzzie piped up.

"Look, Captain, I don't like this. Maybe there's another way."

"There's not," Ritz said. "This-" he gestured at Nakir, "-*thing* seems pretty convinced that I have to do it. So I'll do it. The clock is ticking and I just want to get this over with."

"Nakir," 49 said, turning his attention on the strange being. "If he succeeds, how will he get back?"

"There are one-way gates in the Chamber of Luminescence where the Luminary Heart is. One of them leads back through the arches. But as I said, no living mortal has ever made the journey before."

"Who *has* made the journey?" 49 inquired. "Nakir, why are *you* here exactly."

"I told you, I guard the *Brokk di Fen*. I serve as a guide to those who would travel its path. Without me, all who seek the Luminary Heart would get lost on the path of judgment."

49 nodded, the sun glinting off of his silver head as it bobbed up and down. "How many have you guided through here?"

"Riyaad Tariq will be the first."

This seemed to have a weighted effect on the crew as the words landed. Raquel shifted where she was standing and glanced at Byzzie, who returned her look of concern. 49 remained still as he contemplated something.

"Nakir," he said. "When the network goes down, how will we be able to return home?"

"When you destroy the Luminary Heart, all pathways between what you call the Void Gates will be closed to you."

"Wait," Ritz said. "Are you saying we're stuck here?"

"You have your ship. You may travel as far as it will take you."

"Ha," Byzzie laughed but Ritz saw she wasn't smiling. If anything, she looked close to being sick. "Even at top speed, we would never reach another habitable planet. Not from here. Not in our lifetime."

"There is a way," Nakir said. "I can send you to one location and one location only. But it will cost you something."

"Oh now there's a surprise," Byzzie said. "Go on. What do you want?"

Nakir seemed unperturbed by Byzzie's sarcasm.

"I will ask it of you when the time is right for the need has yet to reveal itself. Until then, you will have to decide where it is you would like to go. I see you. I see your wayward hearts. And I see they are not all pointed in the same direction." Nakir turned toward Ritz and held out a hand. "Are you ready?"

"Is it even possible to be ready?"

"If you step through, then you are. If you do not, then you are not."

Ritz ran a hand through his hair and noticed that it was trembling. He wasn't sure if it was from fatigue, his injuries, or simply from the fear of what he was about to do. Drawing in a deep breath and listening to the soft mechanical buzz of machinery in his chest, he steadied himself.

Then, setting his gaze forward, he walked through the gate.

———

VANESSA WASN'T sure whether she should shoot James, the two PUC soldiers who had just walked in, or herself for being so stupid. She should have taken control the moment that James had walked in after blatantly disregarding orders and doubling back. She could have quietly taken Goff's pistol, shot James, shot Hutchens, and then initiated the rest of her plan.

Hindsight was 20/20 though. There were so many unknown variables at the time—still were, in fact—and she had done the best she could with the knowledge she had. All there was now was to continue on in the same way.

She assessed her situation.

Indigo was under the city and their comms and helmet cams had cut out again. James had just shown himself to be a traitor. Kit was probably already dead. Hutchens and Goff were both wildcards but if she had to choose someone to stand by right now it'd be Goff.

The two PUC soldiers who had just entered had their weapons trained on her and Goff. Goff had his pistol aimed roughly in James's direction. And Hutchens couldn't seem to decide where to aim his.

If Goff was in her corner, which he seemed to be, then they were outnumbered two to three. Even if Hutchens made up his mind and chose her side, it was an even fight, if you could count three regular humans against two regular humans and a super soldier powered by something akin to a nuclear reactor even.

"What are you gonna do James?" Vanessa asked, her voice sounding way more even than she felt. "Kill all of us? You've got a base full of militia members on a planet full of militias. And that's not even counting the seemingly endless hordes of monsters out there. Think this through."

"I have," he said confidently. "I'm not planning on

staying here. The plan is: kill you. Kill anyone who gets in my way as I leave. Kill anyone and *anything* who gets in my way as I huff it back to the transport ship, where I'll meet up with the rest of Indigo. Then get off this shit hole of a planet and set it on fire from space. It's not that difficult. Nebula's dead. The rest of the squads are dead or they'd have made contact by now."

"Why bother?" Vanessa asked. "With us, I mean. You and Indigo could have just fucked off back to the ship when you got in the transport. No need to even go to the hospital if you were planning on this."

"Two reasons," he said. "One, I needed to make sure you were bluffing. I had a feeling you were but if you did somehow have a Light Core under the city and it was somehow hooked up to an orbital defense system, then I didn't want to be caught with my pants down if you somehow found a way to get down there on your own or activate it remotely."

He leaned in and the closer he got the more rounded and distorted Vanessa's image became in his faceplate. "The other reason though—the *real* reason—is because as far as I'm concerned, you were complicit in Joaner's death. You and everyone associated with those traitors. So no, I couldn't just leave. I couldn't just bomb you from space. I have to be here, in front of you. I'm going to look into your dead eyes and then I'm going to go look into Kit's dead eyes. I had to *know* you were dead. But I won't stop there. After we leave this planet we're going to hunt down Nadia and the other scum and wipe them from the face of-"

The door to the comm center whooshed open and James spun on his heel, pistol extended. The two soldiers were caught halfway in the turn when Kit's voice came from the doorway.

"Not another inch." He looked bad. Hunched over and drained of color, he was shirtless from the waist up with two large bandages covering his chest. In his hand, he held a small black pistol and was aiming it square at the nearest soldier's head.

Vanessa adjusted her aim so she had the other soldier in her sights and saw Goff back even further out of the circle, placing both hands on his revolver. Hutchens looked even more flummoxed than before, his pistol bouncing from person to person.

"You better choose wisely," Kit said, jerking his head at the colonel. "Looks like it's an even fight, so it's down to you. Which side you gonna choose?"

"I'm not choosing," Hutchens said through clenched teeth. "If we're gonna make it out of this, everyone in this room needs to be alive. James, stand down."

"Shane's dead then," James said, ignoring Hutchens.

"No, actually. It took some convincing for him to tell me what was up and he'll probably need a hospital bed for a few days. Luckily, one was open."

"Mmm. Lucky." James shrugged his shoulders, the gesture looking far too casual in the bulky Arc Suit. "Guess we better get this over with then, shall we?"

Vanessa saw James's finger begin to tighten on the trigger when Hutchens cried, "Wait!"

Everyone turned to look at him.

"The helmet cams are back on."

"So what?" James snarled.

"So look at what they're picking up."

And Vanessa saw that he was right. The cams were back on. And what they were displaying almost made the gun slip out of her hands.

## 15

# THE DESTRUCTION OF A BODY

Charlene struggled against the rubble with all of her might. Pushing and squirming, there was just enough give around her to work with. Granted, she would have been fighting all the same if her surroundings were completely immovable but that would have been out of a blind, animal panic. Panicking wasn't something that she was prone to but as a rule, most SEUs didn't like the feeling of being trapped and powerless. Whether it was being pinned beneath 600 tons of rubble or flying free and vulnerable through the air in an SEU Drop Pod, the feeling was always one of wretched vulnerability.

There was a loud scraping sound as the rocks around her began sliding apart and she could almost feel the Tesla Arc built into the back of her Arc Suit straining as it dumped nearly inconceivable amounts of energy into her body. Not just to power her arms and legs as she dug her way out but also to facilitate healing from the wound in her abdomen.

The pain of the injury didn't go unregistered but it was definitely secondary to the obstacles before her. It would heal, so long as she didn't sustain any more significant damage and she'd be that much stronger for it.

Charlene felt the whole weight of the accumulated earth shift around her and for a moment she thought it might finish what it had started and slide apart in such a way that would leave her pulverized beneath. Luckily, it didn't.

There was a crack in her Arc Suit's visor and the HUD seemed a bit buggy but all systems were still technically online except for the comms. The mini-map in the upper left of her faceplate was the most important thing, as it both oriented her in terms of the planet's poles and showed her where friendly beacons were. She would need both if she was going to get her crew out of here alive.

Finally standing upright in a large cavern, she noticed that Weaver was already up and moving.

"What's your status, soldier?" Charlene said as she stood up and brushed a coating of dust off of her armor.

Weaver seemed to be dazed but upright. He had his hands on his knees and his right arm was bent at an off-angle.

"Broken arm, I think. Lost my Neural Rifle in the collapse. You?"

"Lost my melee weapon. Cracked visor. Other than that I'm doing okay. I took a penetrating wound up there so that's something we'll have to deal with once we're back onboard a cruiser but nothing we can do about it now. Any idea where Pollie is?"

Weaver stood silently for a moment as he consulted his HUD.

"She's close but there's a lot of interference."

Charlene's HUD told her the same; she had been hoping that it was just her.

"Sorry for dropping a cave on us," Charlene said. "We

were getting overrun so I had to take a chance. Didn't play out as I had hoped."

"The charges aren't that powerful, so it was a good shot," Weaver agreed. "The cave must have been weak."

Charlene gave a curt nod. "Let's see if we can find Pollie."

They searched through the rubble for about a minute, trying to be as quiet and efficient as possible. They didn't exactly know where they were but it was a good bet that at some point the Necrosarks would find them and resume their attack. They wanted to be well on their way out when that happened.

"Hey, I'm getting a weird signal over here," Weaver said as he dislodged a large boulder. "Can you come check this out?"

Charlene stopped where she was digging and joined her teammate. After consulting her HUD, she shook her head.

"Weird," she said. "I got a signal a few feet away. It looks distorted though; it's too big and not the right color."

If Pollie was underneath the rubble then they should just be getting a single blue dot indicating her position. The dot she was looking at though was more like a blob that transitioned from blue to white. She knocked the side of her helmet with her fist to see if it would jar something loose in her display but the image remained.

"Same," Weaver confirmed.

"Let's see what we can do," Charlene said.

They began to dig in the area where the strange signal was coming from and after just a few short seconds they managed to uncover a shattered leg with a white shard of bone sticking out. Judging by the broken armor, it was Pollie.

Charlene felt the back of her throat tighten but continued to dig out the body. When they had finished, they were left holding the pulverized remains of their teammate. It was all in one piece, technically speaking, but both the helmet and chest armor were completely caved in.

The second to die in the last two days. And this one was the direct result of a choice Charlene had made.

They didn't say anything. Weaver simply took the body and moved to carry it on his back. With his broken arm, however, it was clear he was having difficulties and Charlene stepped in to help him. Lifting Pollie's body, she gently rested her so it looked like she was embracing Weaver from behind. There was a soft *thunk* as he engaged the mag locks on his Arc Suit. Then as he stepped away, Charlene confirmed that their fallen sister was secure.

"Hey, look," Weaver said, tilting his head in the direction of where they had retrieved their fallen comrade. In the spot where she had been removed, there was a pulsing purple glow. It was faint but distinguishable in the dark cavern. What was more was that when Charlene checked the mini-map on her HUD, she saw that the distorted signal had been replaced by a crisp white dot.

*No*, Charlene thought to herself. *Not a distorted signal but* two *signals. One for Pollie and the other for...*

"Oh God," Weaver said. "Is that what I think it is?"

"Let's hope not," Charlene said. "But we better check."

Sparing just a few more precious seconds, they dug out more of the area where the purple glow was coming from until there was a four-by-six patch of what looked like thick luminescent magenta skin. The glow seemed to pulse from within and as it did, the skin undulated as if it were the surface of a barely disturbed pond.

Glancing at Charlene for reassurance, Weaver withdrew the black handle of his melee weapon and ignited a blue foot-and-a-half-long plasma blade. Charlene detached her

Neural Rifle from her back, checked its ammunition counter, and readied herself.

There was a loud squelching sound and a gush of fluid as Weaver cut into the strange surface. The truly remarkable thing, however, was that as the hole became wider, they began to hear something like a song coming out of it.

The song was strange and alien, similar to the one she had heard when the first pulse wave had hit. Simultaneously enchanting and revolting, it sounded as if it were played on instruments of living flesh. Euphoria filled her head, followed by a sense of nausea, and then she finally had to fight to keep from vomiting.

"Ugh," Weaver said, rocking where he stood. He stopped cutting for a moment and fought to regain his composure.

As the strange object spilled forth more and more of the viscous substance the song seemed to fade and dissipate into the dank underground air. Charlene stepped back as the liquid pooled and spread out over the ground. Then she bent down and touched it lightly with her finger.

"It doesn't seem acidic," she said. "But try not to get it on your skin. We have no idea what it is."

"Okay," Weaver said as he deactivated his plasma blade and clipped it back on his thigh. He checked his arms to see if he had any breaks in the armor. "Shit, looks like I got a breach on both arms. How about you?"

"I'm good," Charlene replied after checking her own armor. "Let me give it a shot."

Moving quicker now, anxious to get it over with, Charlene stepped up and cautiously submerged her hands in the fluid and fished around. It was hard to get a sense of what she was touching at first but as she continued she gradually confirmed her fears.

Refusing to waste any more time, she plunged her arms

in just a few more inches, grabbed ahold of the thing inside, and wrenched it up and out onto the cavern floor.

"Damn," Weaver said.

"Yup, looks like Gavin."

Gavin Yang was one of the members of White Nebula, the SEU team that had taken point after they had all touched down. They had lost contact with White Nebula just before making it to the medical warehouse in the center of town where they were then picked up by the Leopold, but they had thought their communications had been cut. Not... whatever this was.

The dead SEU lying before them was distinguishable only by the formation of the helmet, which had a unique triangular shape to it. As for the man inside, it looked as if his body had been inflated and was now pushing out through any weak point it could find in his armor. It was hard for Charlene to tell through her visor but the exposed flesh looked deeply bruised and inflamed. The most troubling part though was the pair of dangerous-looking appendages that lay folded at his sides like a couple of collapsable swords.

"What am I looking at?" Weaver said quietly.

"I'm not sure," Charlene answered. "But if I were to guess, it looks like Gavin is being turned into one of those things."

"Why would they need to do that when there's a pulse wave hitting every few hours?"

"Maybe this is their contingency."

"Contingency?" Weaver was incredulous. "They're bugs. Bugs don't have contingencies."

"Nature has built-in contingencies," Charlene said. "Life favors the robust. And these creatures seem to be proving themselves to be more and more robust by the minute."

"Yeah, well this isn't a fucking animal. This isn't nature. This is some sort of monster. A mistake."

Charlene was going to respond when there was a loud chittering from the other side of the cavern. The two SEUs spun, Weaver unclipping his plasma blade and snapping it back on as Charlene shouldered her rifle.

To her relief, she saw that there was only one Necrosark incoming. With two well-placed shots, she sent the creature tumbling and shrieking into the stony floor. Its body lay twitching where it came to rest.

"We need to get out of here," Charlene said urgently.

"Agreed," Weaver said. "What about him?" He gestured at Gavin's body.

"We leave him. I hate to say it but we've already wasted too much time. We need to make it back to the transport and grab James so we can get the hell out of here."

Without needing to be told twice, Weaver reached down and drew his sidearm.

"Let's go."

———

CONCUSSIVE WAVES ROCKED through Ritz as the explosion blew the door out behind him. Hacking and coughing, he spun around just as a bunch of figures, two wearing Marauder armor burst into the room and quickly gunned down the combat synths that had been left there to protect him and everyone else on Kilo Base. But they missed one and just as the heavy robot brought its weapon to bear, one of the invaders, a woman, leveled her small submachine gun and emptied a magazine into it.

Ears still ringing from the explosion, he felt the thrum of gunfire in his guts more than he heard it. Then there was a hot stinging sensation at his neck. It burned and pulsed and when he looked, he saw a thick jet of blood spurt out of him and onto the floor.

A stray bullet. A ricochet.

The world seemed to stand still. Everyone in front of him and around him seemed frozen. Nothing could happen. No one could do anything to save him.

Then something must have happened because gunfire suddenly came alive around him. And not from just one weapon but multiple. More slapping stinging sensations rocked his body and he fell over backwards onto the floor and the last thing he saw was his coworkers of four years hitting the ground beside him.

Chairs careened in every direction as they dropped. Blood splashing. Panicked animal eyes turning and staring into his as the light inside them flickered and went out.

Then for him, there was nothing.


CONCUSSIVE WAVES ROCKED through Ritz as the explosion blew the door out behind him. Then the intruders were in there shooting and he saw Rena go down beside him after taking a round in the neck.

His hands were moving before he even knew what he was doing. He had the gun out of the holster and was bringing it around when his body suddenly came apart in a barrage of bullets and energy rifle fire.

His eyes locked with Rena's as the blood pumped out of her onto the floor.


RITZ EXPERIENCED all of it over and over again. The people in the room dying. Their fear. Their pain. All of the things that could have been for them viciously snubbed out in a single moment of panic and gunfire.

There was something else too. Something he hadn't expected to have had to endure.

After the death of each person, he was then also subjected to the grief of each of the family members as they mourned them upon receiving the news. Then following that grief, he experienced the pain and grief of *those* people's loved ones as it was transferred in the form of impatience, insensitive remarks, and dim morale.

From person to person he jumped. Body to body. And in each new embodiment he endured the endless transference of sin as it was passed from soul to soul like some sort of corrupted gene.

In that time, Ritz lived a trillion lives. He saw the branching effects of a single choice he had made and how it rippled out into the world and—in the suffering that was then dealt back to him—he slowly paid the cosmic debt he had incurred.

And then, when it was all over, he moved on to the next choice. The next sin. And then he lived it all over again.

Oftentimes, certain pathways would overlap. Multiple person's trajectories through life would crossover and in that crossing, the effects of sin would pool together and metastasize. When this happened, the effects would be magnified. A person in some bad situation would be hit with small tragedy after small tragedy in a long series of events, all of which Ritz had had some distant part in.

It was amazing to him how something like a murder could be disarticulated into a million tiny misfortunes over the massive web of human connection but what was more amazing was how a small compromise or misstep in one place could have cascading effects down the line until they had created an unstoppable rolling avalanche.

As the pathways of cosmic treason overlapped and gained momentum, a white lie could become a double homicide. A moment of impatience, a massacre.

It's not that the transgressions would grow by themselves necessarily, but they would combine with others until their cumulative effects were nigh unstoppable. His tiny acts equating to something like a single vote among millions for a ruthless dictator.

There was only one glimmer of light in the whole mess as far as Ritz could tell. Occasionally, the trajectory of a sin would be halted in its tracks. When this happened it was because people took that suffering unto themselves rather than passing it on. They stepped into a gap and helped someone out who was struggling and in doing so, mitigated the damage of the wrongdoing. They would incur the cost themselves whether it cost them time, money, or on some occasions, their very lives.

Ritz had always known this in the abstract. In the Alnabatist Order he had grown up in as a child, he had learned that suffering and hard work were to be carried out dutifully and joyfully, and in doing so, this allowed life to flourish. He had learned that by adhering to one's *fitrah,* or inner sense of right or wrong, they honored Allah and would in turn be blessed with flourishing.

He had also learned that no amount of prayer or religious servitude could stop a bullet.

When he was a child, a group of SEUs had been sent to his village on the planet of Morgiana to retrieve a medicinal plant that grew on the Alnabatist's sacred mountain. The people of his village had offered to slowly mediate out some of the plants for pharmaceutical purposes but the PUC wanted as much as they could as fast as they could get it. When the Alnabatists refused to play ball, the PUC sent in their cold-blooded super-soldiers to get the job done.

Ritz remembered hiding in a tiny compartment in the back of a wardrobe while the rest of his family was rounded up in the living room and executed.

That was the night Ritz learned more about the world than he ever wanted to know.


ONE MOMENT, Ritz was choking to death on his own blood as darkness closed in around him, and the next he was falling face-first onto a smooth black floor. His face hit with a hollow thunk and stars flared in his vision. Shaking off his dizziness and pain, he slowly got to his feet and looked around.

The room he was standing in was a simple square with a doorway behind him and a doorway in front of him. The floor and ceiling were both black and all of the walls were white. Standing just adjacent to the door in front of him was Nakir.

"You have completed the first stretch of your journey," he said.

Ritz rubbed his face with his hands. It felt as if he had just spent the last 4,000 years dying. In a way he had. Probably more, actually, when one considered how many lives he had witnessed.

No, not witnessed. *Inhabited* was closer to the truth. He had inhabited them.

"I don't understand," he said. "Did I really do so much wrong?"

"Yes," Nakir replied. "Though perhaps no more than most others."

"What could I have done to prevent this?"

"Everything. You could have done everything differently. Made different choices. Followed different paths. You did not."

"Then I would have just hurt someone else," he said, gritting his teeth.

"It is likely. But you did not."

"So what?" Ritz said, throwing up his hands. "How am I supposed to act knowing this? How is this supposed to change me?"

"This is not about knowing how to act in the future," Nakir stated. "This is about watching. Being. Enduring. Understanding. This is about justice."

"*Justice?*" Ritz practically spat the word. "How is this justice?"

"It is cosmic justice. All forms of worldly justice are but dim imitations of it. When you hunger for revenge, you want someone to understand what you felt. It does no good if they go to their grave triumphantly with no greater awareness. Revenge only tastes sweet when the one seeking vengeance is allowed to see that dawning realization in their victim's eyes. Even then, it is hollow. It accomplishes nothing. It is the image of Allah that was branded on you and twisted into something destructive. A thing best left to the creator."

"What does that have to do with me?" Ritz asked. "I'm not seeking revenge. I wouldn't even know how to go about finding the ones who killed my family back when I was a kid."

"Every word you have ever uttered has been an arrow aimed at the heart of those who wronged you, Riyaad Tariq. You have harbored hatred and murder in your heart and its tentacles have fastened themselves to everything you've ever touched. While never laying a hand on those who killed your family, you could not keep yourself from reaching out and striking the world."

Nakir fixed Ritz with a hard stare. "Sin is a sickness. And it is communicable."

## 16

## A BURNING FEVER

Charlene took point as she and Weaver attempted to navigate the winding passageways of the dark corridors. Weaver was armed with his pistol and plasma blade but the reach of the Necrosarks tipped the advantage so heavily in their favor that it was preferable for him to simply provide backup. They were not looking to engage the enemy. Now more than ever, they were running.

Slashing limbs emerged from their left and Charlene spun and cut the monster down with a quick burst of rifle fire. There was a skittering out ahead of them and she swung her rifle to deal two more killing shots.

Their numbers were increasing. The amount of Necrosarks they had run across since collapsing the cave was thin but growing. If it kept up at this rate, they'd soon find themselves in the same situation they had tried so desperately to escape from. And without Pollie fighting alongside them, their chances of survival were far slimmer.

"It feels like we're going up," Weaver said.

Charlene saw that he was right, the ground was tilting slowly upward. By falling into another section of tunnel, they must have accidentally accessed some form of exit. She didn't care if the tunnel exited out into the hospital or the city or the bottom of a lake for that matter. She just wanted out.

As soon as they were clear, she would search for the beacon on the transport they had arrived in. Haul ass to it. Then zip over and pick up James. He should be done by then.

Thinking of James, Charlene thought about the comms. They had been down for some time now. Then, as if conjured by magic, there was a hiss of static and the tiny light indicating an open line of communication blinked green.

She almost didn't see it. Wouldn't have, actually, if it hadn't been for the damage done to her helmet. Due to the crack in her visor, she found her eyes constantly refocusing on the screen directly in front of her. The HUD itself wasn't *literally* in front of her—that was tied into her neural network—but the receptors for it were built into her faceplate.

All of that slowly filtered away though, becoming little more than visual background noise. Somewhere miles away, Charlene heard a quick back and forth about the helmet cams being on, which was quickly followed up with a sobering "Oh my God..."

*Oh my God* was right, Charlene thought to herself.

The two SEUs had just rounded a corner and come grinding to a halt. Stretching out before them was a huge antechamber roughly five times the size of the one they had originally fallen into. But this one was radically different.

Hanging all over the ceiling and walls were massive purple pods like the one they had found Gavin in, each with the dark silhouette of a body inside. The stone walls were completely covered with what looked to be an inflamed-looking bright red resin that pulsed and undulated slowly, making it appear as some Hellish cathedral. All throughout the space, there was a low audible hum that seemed to be flirting with some sort of melody.

Centered in the middle of the whole scene was a Necrosark.

It was massive. At least ten times bigger than the others, it also had twice as many legs and a massive bulbous head festooned with countless white eyes and a long vertical mouth that looked to be accented by four pairs of lethal-looking black mandibles.

Charlene watched as a long tentacle snaked its way out of somewhere on the thing's back and slithered down the wall toward a body Charlene had yet to notice until now.

Not wasting any time, the massive Necrosark quickly brought the comatose person to its mouth and began to spin it in a cocoon. Something like a thick purple mucous gushed from its mouth as it worked, the material becoming dense and elastic almost immediately. Finally, the huge insectile monstrosity used one of its impossibly long limbs to reach over and secure the pod to the ceiling.

"I think we've seen enough here," Charlene said. Then she raised her rifle, lining up the targeting reticle with the monster's quivering face and pulled the trigger.

———

"THEY'RE BREEDING," Vanessa said, staring slack-jawed at the screen.

"More than that," Hutchens added. "They're definitely the ones blocking our comm signal."

"How do you figure?" Vanessa looked over at him, the tense stand-off in the room momentarily forgotten.

"Didn't you notice the slight interference? There's a sort of static on the screen."

"So?" Vanessa said, but then she got it. Looking closer now, she saw that the static seemed to increase and decrease along with the slow pulsing of the red resin that coated the walls.

"Ah, I see," she said slowly. "At first I thought it was just regular interference, but..."

"But what?" James's voice boomed behind her.

"But they're slightly out of rhythm," Hutchens explained. "It's slight but if you watch long enough you can see it. It's not a glitch in the system; the system is reacting to it somehow."

Vanessa was nodding slowly to herself. "Whatever that chamber is, it seems to have found a way to localize the pulse wave that creates those things. It's almost subsonic but I think the light pulses are increasing in tempo. It probably hits a crescendo at some point and bursts, knocking down all of the comms."

"Why is it so random then? Sometimes it goes down for a minute, sometimes an hour."

"Maybe it has something to do with the amount of bodies in the room," Vanessa wondered out loud. "Maybe those purple pods affect it."

While they were speaking, Vanessa felt James's eyes silently boring into her. Even behind his dense faceplate, it was there. She was being watched. Assessed. She decided to shut up.

Too late.

"I get it." James looked at the screen and then back at Vanessa. "That's why you wanted my team to go down there.

You didn't want to kill us, you wanted to gather intel. You wanted eyes on the enemy."

Vanessa didn't answer. Hutchens eyed both of them. A heavy click cut through the air as Goff cocked his revolver and the two PUC soldiers tensed in turn, causing Kit to step forward and place the muzzle of his pistol against the nearest one's head. James turned his attention toward Kit and leveled his own pistol at the battered Marauder's face.

"I killed the guy," Kit said casually. "The one that was supposed to kill me. He's dead, isn't he?"

After no one answered, Hutchens took it upon himself. "He's dead. No one blames you for that, Kit."

"I'm just trying to figure out if I blame *myself* for that." Kit's tone was conversational, undercutting the tension in the room. "You know, I left the PUC because I didn't want to take another human life. Not ever again. I've spared those who probably didn't deserve it and went to painstaking lengths not to hurt anyone. Then in the 11th hour..." He shrugged. "I'm just who I was before I went AWOL. Like I had been occupied by some other person for that short period of time between leaving and now."

"Are you saying you're not going to kill any of us?" James said wryly. "Because that would be extremely helpful."

"No," Kit answered. "I might. What I'm saying is that I don't really know who I am anymore. I just reacted in a way that was completely counter to who I thought I was. It's strange."

"A peculiar time to be waxing philosophical, bud," Goff said grimly.

"I'm not entirely sure I'll be walking away from this one," Kit replied. "I'm not in the greatest of shape right now, so I just want to get some things straight first."

"And?" Goff asked. "What's it looking like? I

would *very* much like to know what you're going to do." He waved his gun toward Hutchens. "See if you can get an answer out of him too while you're at it."

"How about I just decide for you." James cut in.

And the room exploded in gunfire.

————

RITZ FELL through endless eons of time, his body coming apart and being stitched back together over and over again. He lived life-after-life and suffered death-after-death. As his journey progressed, his mind slowly became something other than a human mind. His body became something low and ground down, despite its constant revival. It seemed to be having some invisible part of it stripped away, some ligament of the soul that was becoming worn and threadbare as it was gradually digested by the accumulated suffering of a cursed world.

By the time he reached the final stretch, he felt something else entirely. Were he able to articulate the feeling, he would have said that there was simply no part of him left to damage. No essential piece that could further disintegrate against the sawtooth edge of existence as it whipped by him on its fatal path.

He was wrong.

There was still something. An essential lie that held him together like the final support beam of a collapsing building. He knew that if this structure were to fail, so would he. His entire existence would cave in on itself, any sense of having bettered the world on his own merit finally put to death.

But there it was: the inevitability. Since facing his first sin here, in this place where reality was finally laid bare before him, he knew that he would come to this final scene. This final act that made him nothing more than an animal in his own mind.

He crouched there shivering in the room, listening to the steady pop of single-shot gunfire. It was infrequent but seemed to be getting closer, each shot louder than the next. He wrapped his arms around his wife and children. They had been trying to hold it together since the terrorists had arrived. Nowhere to run. No one to call. They just hid and prayed they would be passed over.

Susie, Finn, and Tracy didn't know what was happening. Especially Tracy, who had just turned two last month. The memory of the small celebration they had had as a family lodged itself in the center of Ritz's mind. They had made a small cake out of bread flower, water, baking soda, and sugar. The batter had been flat and deflated so they had had to make what amounted to a bunch of pancakes that they then stacked and covered in a sweet white frosting.

Tracy hadn't cared. It was special to her. The first birthday she could come close to appreciating. He remembered her face and shirt covered in the thick frosting as she tried jamming another piece into her mouth, her large brown eyes searching her parents' faces for approval.

There was a loud bang and a spear of light stabbed into the dark room. The door swung open and everyone huddled closer together. Ritz had no words now. He wanted to beg but his throat wouldn't work so he begged with his eyes.

Another figure appeared by the door and there was a short exchange. Ritz could barely make out the hushed words but it sounded like they were trying to decide what to do with them. Finding his courage, he worked his throat, trying to conjure the words. But before he could, the man leveled the rifle and pulled the trigger.

The gun screeched like the tearing of sheet metal. It resonated with the very cry of his soul and as it screamed, he felt the small bodies in his arms crumble apart into pieces as wet and sorrowful as falling tears.

LIGHT FLASHED by Ritz as he was catapulted into another mysterious room. This one also had white walls and a black ceiling and floor, but before him now stood a golden door. The edges of the frame rippled with purple light.

Standing next to the door was Nakir. He reached out a hand.

"The final lie is dispensed with," he said.

Ritz reached up and touched his face. His eyes stung. His head was pounding. He felt as if any slight movement would cause him to crumble into dust.

"It wasn't me," he cried, but he knew it wasn't true. Nakir just looked on. "It wasn't..." But he couldn't get the rest of the words out. His face contorted as he fell backward, his legs tucked beneath him in a flat kneeling position. His body began to writhe of its own accord and he felt his feet come out from under him as he rolled onto his side.

"You know the truth now," Nakir said. "And it is a part of you. Any sin that pairs itself with a lie has its power doubled and is yet that much weaker for it. But the lie is not yet dead. For a lie is a hydra with many heads. You have removed them but now you must cauterize the wounds. Only you can keep those heads from growing back."

"How?"

"Say it."

"But I-"

"Say it."

Ritz felt his lips and tongue moving, seemingly

disconnected from his brain. As if the timeless journey he had embarked on so long ago had turned his body against his own rational thought and was moving it towards something as painful as it was cleansing.

"I killed them," he said. "Goff told me to but I was the one who pulled the trigger. And when I did it, I didn't feel bad, I felt...relief. I was relieved that I wouldn't have to watch my back for the rest of my life, afraid that someone from that family would go point the authorities at me. Relieved that, if pressed by anyone, I could blame Goff. Say that he gave the order."

Ritz felt relief now. Not the relief that comes with removing a stone from one's back but by adding one.

"There is one more thing you must see," Nakir said. And he showed him.

Ritz watched as if in a dream. Formless and without perspective now, he saw it all unfold. The other reality. The other confluence of events. The one where Tracy, the youngest of the family he had murdered, grew up. Where she developed a heart for freedom and action. Scorning the brutal tactics of the other militias, she was privileged enough to have connections within the PUC through her husband. Slowly but surely, they built a secret coalition within the current government and eventually overturned and replaced the current rulers. It was a long shot, one that only a person in her position with her connections could do, but one that Ritz now saw was possible.

"After sparing them, you would have continued to work with Kingsbane instead of losing your taste for it as you had. The crew of the Leopold would have never been formed. You would have never gotten lost while fleeing from Kilo Base and 49 and Mary's Burden would have drifted on in darkness until thousands of years later."

"What about the Light Wire Network?" Ritz asked.

Byzantine Jackson would have remained with her family on Desia and discovered the plot to establish a Light Wire before it came to fruition. The invasion would have still taken place but in the form of a covert war where the PUC sought to establish a base and Desia sought to undermine it. This would then last until the eventual takeover from within by Tracy Stephenson. Once Tracy found out about this plot to undermine the peace and independent authority of the Pillon System she would then put a stop to it."

Ritz's mind was swimming. All of the memories of the deaths he had endured since passing through the gateway. All of the pain and rippling consequences. It was so big that he had almost lost control of any form of linear thought. Even here, where his flesh and blood weren't bound by the same constraints as that in the real world, he struggled to hold on. To remember.

His mind suddenly stumbled upon a question.

"What about Raquel?" he asked.

"Raquel. You are asking what happened to her in this other reality."

"Yes."

Nakir stood there, the strangely inhuman face implacable.

"Raquel remained at the PUC facility," he finally said. "She remained there for 13 years 4 months and 17 days before her heart gave out and she died."

Ritz clenched and unclenched his teeth, trying to force his thoughts to lineup.

"And you weigh her life as less than the others?" Ritz asked.

"You misunderstand, Tariq. This is not about what should have happened. It is about what could have happened. A possible future were certain choices have been made. Your judgment isn't about me showing you things, it's about you seeing them. Feeling them. Experiencing them. I see that your faculties are but a thread, which is to be expected. I shall therefore commence the last step of the journey."

"And what is that?"

"The rest."

"The rest of what?" Ritz didn't think he could take a literal step forward, let alone whatever Nakir had in store for him.

"The rest of all other possible realities."

Before Ritz could react to this, Nakir stepped forward and touched his forehead, sending the visions of infinite possible realities shuttling through the core of his being. And what was left of him after could truly no longer be called human.

THERE WAS NO DOOR NOW. No black and white room. The ethereal essence of Riyaad Tariq drew toward the Luminary Heart, and were he to see it as a man sees things, it would have appeared to him as a pulsing organ beating in an unsteady arrhythmia as ultraviolet light coursed through it. He knew that it was sick with infection. With *Port ek Thall*. Poison from the Void. He reached out and grasped the beating heart, ready to crush it.

Then he stopped.

What would happen if he destroyed the heart while the Poison from the Void was still infecting it? It would have to go somewhere else, but where? He thought about all he had experienced in this strange place, about the way pain and suffering seemed to spread even as people tried to grind it out.

After a final moment of contemplation, Ritz felt his mind stretch out like an elastic dough and absorb the infection. Were he to see it, he may have envisioned a cup of dark liquid that he then drank in a single draft.

It burned with heavy black fire. The center of him sunk down and then rebounded, dark webs of suffering turning from black to purple and finally into a deep blue. The agony turned into sorrow. It was unbearable. Feeling impossibly anxious and hurried, he sought a place to dump it.

The Network. Back into the connection. No, he couldn't.

With all of his might, he rolled that heavy sorrow into a ball, reached out and clutched the network connecting all of space and then ripped it from existence like a scab.

Soundlessly and without end, he screamed. He screamed and stumbled and searched for an escape.

The gateway. The stone arch. He saw it.

Something in him strained and gave way as he moved toward it. There was a snap and then he was passing through to the other side, that heavy sorrowful poison pulling him down, down, down.

———

IN THE GLADE, on the other side of the stone arch, there was a snap and a flash of light and everyone saw Ritz step back through the gateway less than a second after he had entered. He stood there frozen for a single moment, and then his body melted to the ground in a red sludge.

No one said anything. Then Raquel started to scream.

## 17

## THE BELT

When the smoke cleared and the final droplets of misted blood had settled on the surfaces of the comm center, Vanessa Jackson tried to come to terms with what had just happened.

As far as she could tell, the first person to fire their weapon had been Goff, the massive handgun booming in his hand. A red glob of plasma and lead streaked across the room and sent James stumbling back, a burning hole in his armor. The next shot had come from Vanessa's own pistol, hitting the soldier on the right in the neck. Then everyone was shooting.

At some point, Kit had shot the other soldier in the back of the head and the dying man had let loose a spray of energy rifle rounds, one of which had seared Vanessa's left ear off and another that caught Hutchens in the gut, roughly where he had been wounded by the Necrosark earlier.

Goff was aiming his pistol for a second shot but James's enhanced body had already regained its composure. But instead of aiming at his attacker, the SEU pointed his pistol at Kit and pulled the trigger. The tiny bullet caught Kit in the forehead and spat his brains out onto the door behind him. It slid open with a gentle whoosh as he collapsed backward.

Before Kit hit the ground, Goff squeezed off his second shot, this time hitting James just below the chin. The SEU's head rolled sideways and then toppled off his shoulders entirely.

The entire sequence of events had happened in less than three seconds and now Vanessa was standing there holding a hand to the side of her head where her ear had been, the smell of blood and burnt ozone heavy in the air. There was a groan and she turned to look at Hutchens who fell out of his chair, gun clattering to the floor.

"Ah shit," the colonel grated. He took a hand away from his stomach, revealing it to be slick with blood. He put it back.

"Get a medic," he said. "We should have at least one of my guys standing by."

Vanessa ignored him and stepped up to the console.

The screen displayed absolute chaos. She watched as Charlene smashed the butt of her rifle into an attacking Necrosark's face and then proceeded to gun it down as it stumbled backward. Looking over just in time, Vanessa saw two huge mandibles fill the other screen and heard Weaver give little more than a grunt before his helmet cam cut out. Charlene's cam snapped sideways to reveal Weaver being lifted into the air as he brought the white plasma blade up into the monster's jaw again and again.

There was a wet crunch and the SEU's headless body fell limply to the ground.

Charlene still seemed to be holding her own, until a jagged limb came seemingly out of nowhere and disappeared where her neck should have been. The sounds of gunfire persisted even as they were accompanied by the gurgling sound of Charlene's helmet quickly filling with her own blood.

The last surviving member of Indigo Squad turned her gaze upward and the giant wounded Necrosark filled the screen, its massive body stretched out over the ceiling festooned with hanging purple pods. Half of its face had been torn away, along with a number of its eyes. But the ones that were left seemed to be staring through Charlene, through the screen, and through Vanessa. What it saw there, she couldn't say.

Then the heart monitor on Charlene's HUD went flat.

"Did you hear me?" Groaned Hutchens from the floor.

Vanessa continued to ignore him as she punched in a command on the console. She looked over at Goff who was watching her actions very closely. He was still holding the large pistol in his hand.

"Ya know, Colonel," she said, turning back to the screen. "You were right about the Light Core. You were just wrong about where it was." She tapped a few more keys and hit send. "You're actually about 300 feet above it. And as far as Glenhold is concerned, well. I've got something there but it ain't no Light Core." She hit the keys two more times. "Remember how you theorized Desia was a trap?"

She turned toward the fallen colonel, who stared back at her.

"Funny you didn't apply that to Glenhold as well." There was a *clack* as she hit the final button on the computer console and a deep rumble sounded from far off in the distance as the entire cave system Glenhold was built over collapsed into flames, taking the city with it.

The colonel's face had gone so pale it was bordering on

translucent. It looked like he was trying to form a complicated question but ended up just settling on, "Why?"

"Why burn the city?" Vanessa asked. "I had certainly hoped there would be more PUC there when I hit the button but I'll take what I can get."

"We could have been allies," he hissed. "We could have put this ridiculous war behind us. We could have built a new world."

"That's the thing. I don't want the world you want. I don't want another PUC to babysit me. I don't want your security. Your protection. Because in the end, it just all amounts to the same thing." Vanessa reached down and unbuckled her belt, the one Byzzie had given her for the job. Her contribution to the act.

She watched Hutchens as the man's eyes drifted down to what she was doing and then back up.

"And what's that?" he said shaking his head. Anger in his eyes now. Frustration.

Vanessa strode around behind the man. He tried to turn but she kicked him in the shoulder and he fell forward. Falling to her knees and straddling him from behind, she whipped the belt around his neck and began to pull.

"My babies," she rasped, feeling hot tears sting her eyes for the first time. Finally. Gloriously. She felt the grief flow through her. "Dead. In the street. With no one around to even bury the bodies."

She pulled harder as Hutchens clawed at his neck. He tried kicking and thrashing but he was too weak. She pulled even harder.

"Well, let me tell you," she said. "They're buried now."

Vanessa stared at the back of the man's head, her fists clenched so tight she began to feel the leather cut into her skin. The side of her head roared from the rifle round that had taken her ear and she used it. Let it surge through her and give her strength.

Then, the colonel's rigid body thrashed a final time, tensed, and slackened. Vanessa held on for three more minutes, eyes clenched shut, then finally let the belt slacken. There was a hollow *thunk* as the dead man's head hit the floor.

After wiping her eyes, Vanessa finally looked up at Goff who was quietly assessing her. She spoke first.

"Grab one of the rifles on the floor." Her voice felt hoarse and weary but not without authority. "Gather your men. Sweep the base. Kill anyone in a PUC uniform."

"What about the fleet?" Goff asked.

"It'll be taken care of."

Resolve hardened the large man's features. There was a loud clack as he flipped the cylinder open on his revolver. He popped the spent shells out and pocketed them, then replaced them with fresh cartridges and pushed the cylinder back in. After holstering the weapon, he walked over and picked up one of the fallen soldier's energy rifles. He reloaded that as well then glanced back at Vanessa.

She was back at the computer console, typing in the commands and security clearance to pull up the ground-to-orbit cannons. He looked like he was going to say something, but then he evidently changed his mind and chose instead to simply nod. The door to the comm center slid open and he stepped carefully over Kit's body as he exited.

Once the door was shut, Vanessa turned to look at Kit. His body was twisted at an odd angle, blank eyes staring just over her shoulder as if something in a different world, in a different life were approaching from behind.

She felt a pang of sadness and regret. The man had

saved her life and been a friend of her daughter's. What would she think? What would any of them think when they came back here to discover what she had done?

Byzzie knew some of it, of course, but not the details. She knew that Hutchens was going to die and could probably infer from that the fate of the rest of his men. Beyond that, however?

Vanessa closed her eyes and took a moment to compose herself. She let her mind touch lightly on the grief she felt deep down inside of her. The grief and the fear.

Then, feeling something harden within her, she reached down and proceeded to blow the remnants of the PUC fleet out of the sky.

## 18

## THE WAY FORWARD

It was done. The Void Gates had been disabled. The web connecting the galaxy, removed. The pulse wave that had created the Necrosarks, put to a stop. They had succeeded.

They had succeeded but all Raquel could think about was the look on Ritz's face before he was liquefied in front of them. It was horrible. Truly horrible. Raquel would have thrown up if she hadn't been screaming so hard. Now that she had stopped, she felt the back of her throat roll and thought she still might.

There was a crack and Nakir descended down into the middle of the glade. The crew of the Leopold had gathered together in the seconds since Ritz had died and Nadia had regained consciousness soon after that. The Marauder was now standing tall, back rigid, rifle clutched tightly in both hands.

There was something there though that Raquel couldn't quite put her finger on. An uncertainty in her posture. As if she had never been so ready to fight in her life but had nothing to fight against.

"The network is down," Nakir said. "The Void Gates are no more."

"And the Necrosarks? They're gone?"

"They remain," Nakir answered. "And they have found a way to reproduce. The method is slower and more localized but they will continue to multiply."

"What?" Byzzie looked frantically around. "Then why the fuck are we here? This was for nothing."

"Their reproduction is slowed," Nakir stated for a second time. "It is easier to get your house together in a rainstorm than a hurricane, would you not agree?"

"I don't-" Byzzie began, but 49 cut her off.

"Ritz," the android looked over at the unsightly wet puddle at the base of the stone arch. "Is he..."

"His body was destroyed. The cosmic judgment proved too much for his flesh to handle."

"Why do I get the feeling you knew that would happen?" Byzzie asked.

"I did not know. But I suspected."

"Oh bull-"

"The light is waning," Nakir said. "I will bring you where you ask but you must ask now. My power to do so is but the lingering twilight of a sun already set."

They all looked at each other. They had had virtually no time to discuss the matter. For them, Ritz had only been gone for a moment.

Raquel wanted desperately to say, *home. My home, wherever that is.* But she didn't. She couldn't. To make such a decision for the rest of them...

"What about Desia?" Nadia asked. The question was directed at the crew.

"Yeah, I second that," Marcus said, speaking up for the first time. Samantha was nodding next to him.

"Wait…" Byzzie said, surprising them. After all, if anyone wanted to go back to Desia, it should have been her. "What's happening there?" She shifted. "I mean, do they need us?"

"What a person needs is not for me to decide," Nakir said. "Much less a whole planet. But what you have conceived in your heart has come to fruition, Byzantine Jackson. Kurt Hutchens is dead. Only the inhabitants of Desia remain in the dwelling where you sought shelter."

"What?" If a robot could look confused, 49 was doing a damn good job. "What do you mean dead? How?"

"My mom," Byzzie said, her voice low. "We talked about it before I left. She invited me to be a part of it. I gave her the belt she said she'd do it with."

"Do it with?" 49 said. "Do *what* with?"

"Kill Hutchens. She said she was going to strangle him until his face was purple and his feet stopped kicking. She wanted to bring him and the entire PUC occupation down. She was never going to work with them and they were never going to work with her. And even if she tried, the rest of Desia wouldn't have done it. Not ever. Not after what they brought to our doorstep."

49 looked troubled. Everyone looked troubled, actually. And Raquel would have been too if she wasn't so distracted. Finally, she couldn't hold it in any longer. She asked the question.

"Sorry, guys. Before we decide where to go I need to ask Nakir a question." She glanced over at 49, made eye contact, and then glanced back. "Can you tell me how to get somewhere."

49 stepped forward. "Yes, here are the coordinates." He reached out his hand and a long sequence of numbers sprang to life at the end of his fingertips. They hovered in midair, illuminated by the Light Core.

Nakir strode slowly over and looked at it.

"These coordinates," he said. "Where did you get them?"

49 turned toward Raquel. "From her."

Nakir seemed to be reassessing Raquel, his stark razor-sharp features standing out like some ancient mechanism whose meaning and purpose had been forgotten.

"Did you come from here?" Nakir asked.

Raquel saw something in him flex. There was a rippling in the skin. A sharpening of the eyes. The air around him seemed to heat up.

"I don't know," Raquel answered truthfully. "I just woke up on Lithoway, by a river."

"By a river." Nakir's gaze seemed to be piercing her. Probing her. Searching for something. Raquel got the distinct feeling that, were she to move, she might suddenly never move again.

"Yes."

"Why?" 49 broke in. "What's strange about these coordinates?"

"They are for here," Nakir answered. "Or they almost are."

"Are you saying I came from this place?" Raquel asked, looking around. The mountain, the trees, the thin sky overhead. If she had come from here then she didn't remember any of it.

"Almost." Nakir stepped up and placed a warm hand on Raquel's cheek, fixing her with his stare. He took his hand away.

"Those are not the coordinates for this *exact* place. Not quite." He lifted a hand and pointed at a single number a third of the way through the line of code. "There should be another number, right there."

"What does that mean?" Raquel asked.

"It is a shadow of this place," Nakir explained. "There are no truly bad things in the world, only good things that have been corrupted. This is one such place. It is what you see before you but twisted. I have long suspected that such a place existed but it has been shielded from me."

Nakir turned and began to pace, looking for the first time to be truly uneasy.

He stopped and turned toward Raquel. "I would have you go there."

"What?" Raquel felt her chest tighten. Some nauseous mix of uncontrollable excitement and dread seemed to flow from her head down into her toes and fingertips.

"I cannot send you there, however. The way is blocked before me but I can drop you in its respective galaxy. From there you must find it yourself."

"Wait, wait, wait," Samantha cut in. "Are we going to this place now? What about Desia?"

"This is the request I spoke of earlier. It has revealed itself to me and though your passage into the Luminary Chamber has already taken place, I cannot demand it. Not something like this. So I ask: do this for me and you can go anywhere."

"If we do this," Samantha said. "Then how will you transport us to Desia afterward? It sounds like your ability to do so is fading as we speak. Am I wrong?"

"You are not wrong. But the location I would have you venture to has a tunnel."

"A tunnel," 49 said. "Do you mean a Void Tunnel?"

"Yes," Nakir replied. "While the gates are closed, the tunnels remain for they are true tears in the fabric of space. Most existed before what you call the Dislocation. It will not bring you directly to the Pillon System but there is a route you may take."

"I don't know," Samantha was shaking her head.

"You may do this," Nakir said. "But you must decide as a group. You cannot go to two places. As has been pointed out, my ability to transport you anywhere at all is growing thinner by the minute."

"Let's decide then," 49 said, all business. "Where to? Let's take a vote. Nakir, what's this place called?"

"*Forn Raktanna,*" Nakir said.

"*Forn Raktanna.*" 49 said the words back and at first, they sounded strange to Raquel. She couldn't tell why, exactly, but as she observed the robot, she noticed that he had become stock-still as if in some sort of stasis.

"Yes," Nakir said. "You are aware of this place?"

"In a way," 49 said, never sounding as robotic as he did right now. "It is called the Range of Spears by those who found it. But it is known as *Forn Raktanna* in an older tongue, which translates roughly into *Silver Teeth.*"

"That is correct," Nakir said. "By wind and rumor it has troubled my heart, my soul, and my mind."

"And you'd like us to go there?" Byzzie asked, raising her eyebrows.

"What you have done today is no small thing," Nakir answered. "And I stated before that I would ask you for something in return."

"I think we already gave something," Nadia said dangerously, jerking her head in the direction of the puddle that used to be Ritz.

"A man can give his life and no one else's," Nakir explained. "Tariq could not live here in this world after what he experienced. What I ask of you is altogether different."

"How?" Byzzie challenged.

"I cannot accompany you, for one. There are places that are closed off to me in the way a fish is barred from living in a desert. And the task will not be without its peril. I suspect there is some force that dwells among those mountains. I have not seen it. But I have sensed something like a restlessness behind my eyes. Far off, something slithers in the dark."

"You're really selling it," Byzzie said. "Tell me this: why were you willing to let us pick our own destination a few minutes ago but now we're apparently going on this little expedition of yours?"

Nakir moved in closer to Byzzie and the young girl involuntarily shrunk back.

"I tolerate you because your path is etched in the lines of this world's salvation. But do not overstep. I am no mere mortal with which to trade veiled curses. I am a celestial body that serves the First Light—the light by which all things are seen. My will is bound to the shifting currents of fate, as are my requests."

"So what's to keep you from changing your mind again?" Byzzie asked, her tone notably subdued.

"Nothing," Nakir said. "For our fates are now entwined. But this is hardly new to you humans. Your paths and futures are ever-shifting like dunes of sand. I may yet ask you to fall in and devour each other. You would certainly have the choice not to do so. And I would then exercise my own choice in turning you into an atomized sludge."

Everyone was quiet.

"I'll go," Raquel said. "If we're taking a vote, I vote to go."

"Me too," 49 said. "I was once a servant of the Black Tongue and the Silver Teeth. My past lies there, as does my future."

Raquel looked to Byzzie and she nodded.

"What about Amelia and King?" Samantha said. "We should ask them too."

"There is no time," Nakir declared. "You must decide *now*. In fact, you have one minute. I can't make you go anywhere but I can leave you here."

"But what about Kit?" Nadia said. "How will we-"

"He is dead and so is his murderer," Nakir said quickly. "He died trying to save Vanessa Jackson and killed a man in the process. The cost to him was great."

Nadia stood there, shocked. Raquel didn't know what to say. Kit? Dead? It was too much. Everything was happening too fast.

"We'll go," 49 said. "That is my decision. Anyone who wishes to stay here may do so. This is where our fight lies."

"Wait," Marcus said, looking from the android to Samantha.

"I will drop you at the edge of the system," Nakir said. "From there, however, you must find your own way. The system itself is unnamed. If any have traveled there they have done so only by mistake and misfortune. As its form is shielded from me, I know not how deep nor how vast it is. I bid you luck."

And before they could get another word in, they were swallowed whole by a wave of white light.

# EPILOGUE

The ocean breeze blew across the yard, bringing with it the scent of salt. The day was warm and everyone was outside. Children chased each other in the grass while a few adults sat at a wooden table. Others were inside cooking the afternoon meal.

A woman in purple sat listening to an older man tell a story. She nodded along, twirling her dark brown hair in her fingers.

"Raquel," another woman yelled through an open window.

The woman in purple tilted her head. Turning to excuse herself, she smiled, her eyes cast down. Once on her feet, she reached down and grabbed her walking stick.

The woman from the window called again. Raquel tilter her head a second time, orienting herself. Then, tapping her stick out in front of her, she walked slowly across the yard.

THERE WAS no vomit this time when Raquel awoke. The ceiling of her living quarters swam into focus above her. She raised her fingers to her face and felt tears. The dream had been so real. Like a memory. Disembodied, she had seen herself stand and walk across the yard.

She was blind. Or at least, she was in whatever world she entered when she passed through the Void. What did it mean? Why could she see here? Were these memories or something else?

The ship hummed gently around her and she lay there. The feeling of that place—it felt like...what?

Like home.

She had no memories of the yard and the house and of the people beyond what she saw in the Void, yet they still brought up some feeling of deep nostalgia within her. She closed her eyes, letting the afterglow continue to wash over her.

---

NADIA SAT at the helm while the rest of the crew got some well-deserved rest. They had all woken up in their quarters as if they had never visited the Gaia Spine. There was even a part of Nadia that believed they hadn't—that wanted to think they had just had some sort of Void dream like Raquel often had.

But there was still the ache in her bones from where Nakir had knocked her unconscious. And they were still missing Ritz.

Nadia leaned back, closing her eyes. Ritz was gone. God, Kit was gone. Losing Ritz was painful but losing Kit was something else. It felt like she was drowning—caught in a nightmare that refused to let go. The whole reason she was here was because of Kit. She tried to care about the crew's mission but to her it was too external. Too ill-defined.

So they wanted to fight the PUC. Sure, fine. But to what end? To stop war? To stop pain? Suffering? All those things would still be there. She had a hard time getting ahold of it. She had never seen it as her place to question a mission, but what they were striving for here seemed unattainable. And now that Ritz was gone would they continue forward?

Nadia heard the tell-tale click of a pair of crutches approaching the door to the bridge. A normal person wouldn't have been able to pick it up, but with her enhanced hearing, she could hear a cough all the way from the crew quarters if the ship was quiet enough.

A few seconds later, the door swished open behind her.

"Something I can do for you, King?"

He looked at her, still in obvious pain. Without saying a word he went and slumped down in the corner, leaning his crutches up beside him. He took a few deep breaths.

At first, she thought he wasn't going to answer her. Then he shook his head. "I feel like it's just me now."

Nadia didn't respond. When it came to people to talk to on the ship, King was relatively low on the list. The man was often too gruff at times, alluding to things without saying them. Simultaneously over-emotional and emotionally cut off. The fact that he was here and wanted to talk—and talk to her, no less—was surprising.

"When we started, it was just Ritz and Hector and I," he said. "Three guys breaking away from Kingsbane. Now Ritz and Hector are gone. I'm the only one left."

"No you're not," Nadia said. "We're all here. We're in this together." It seemed like the right thing to say.

King raised his eyebrows and gave her a soft but penetrating look. "We're all here," he repeated back at her. "We're all in this together. Do you believe it?"

Nadia thought about that for a moment, then answered truthfully. "I do."

"Good. I'm glad," he said. "What are you feeling right now?"

"Excuse me?"

"Kit's gone." He said gently. "What are you feeling?"

Nadia thought about that. She thought about the answer and then whether or not she should reveal this part of herself to King.

"I feel..." She shifted uncomfortably. "Bad."

Hell, how had he turned this on her? She was supposed to be the one prying him open, not the other way around.

He laughed. "Ya don't say? C'mon, you can do better than that."

Nadia took a moment to think.

"Powerless," she finally admitted. "I'm the strongest person on this ship but I still feel...helpless. Like there's nothing I can do." She felt something twinge behind her eyes. Her throat tightened. "And I feel...like I'm alone now."

King nodded.

"Like, I've lost some part of myself. Like an actual body part. But worse. I'd rather lose my arm or leg. Or my life." She nodded to herself. "I would rather have lost my life."

"There are some people that are greater extensions of ourselves than our actual bodies," King said. "You know me, I'm an individualist. But we are not merely individuals. We are also the people around us—the people we love. When they die, a piece of them stays with us, but a piece of us also leaves with them."

Nadia was silent as she thought about Kit. About the future and the different paths she could have taken. If it wasn't for Kit, she'd still be with the PUC. She'd feel fulfilled. She'd feel...not like this.

"I can't stop thinking about what his last moments must have been like," she said. "Nakir said he killed a man. I wasn't there for him and he killed a man."

"What do you mean?" King asked.

"He hated that. Killing. He wanted to help. He wanted to use his skills to incapacitate, not kill. That was a beautiful part of him and I fought to preserve it. I didn't agree with him but I didn't want him to ever lose that piece of himself."

"You're saying that if you could have been there, on Desia, you could have been the one to kill that man and not him."

Nadia shrugged. "I don't know. I just...failed him. Completely."

"Do you think he'd say that?"

"No," Nadia answered. "He was too kind."

"He was kind but he wasn't a liar," King said. "You did what you did because of who you are. You thought you were making the right choice by helping us shut down the Light Wire Network. That's all you can do. Learn and move on."

"Look what learning cost me," Nadia said.

"Learning and love," King said. "Those are the two things in this world that cost the most. But without them, we're nothing. Today you paid the price of being human."

They were silent a long time. The black slid calmly by the viewport, star-speckled and unassuming.

Nadia thought about where they were going. If the navigation system on the Leopold was to be believed, it would be months before they reached the Range of Spears and who knew what lay in their path.

She looked over at King, intending to ask how he felt—what his intentions were now that Ritz was gone. But he had fallen asleep.

*Crimes of the Blood Cults*

*The Omen Tree*

# ABOUT THE AUTHOR

Fredrick Niles is the author of *Ash Above, Snow Below* and *The Omen Tree*. He lives in St. Paul, Minnesota where he writes fiction and plays music. In his free time he rants about movies, lurks in bookstores, and practices introversion with his wife.

facebook.com/fredricknilesauthor
instagram.com/fredrickniles_author

www.ingramcontent.com/pod-product-compliance
Lightning Source LLC
Chambersburg PA
CBHW030630190726

48286CB00008B/2470